# Blue Man

Published by Tova Dian Dean

# Table of Content

# Chapter One

Julian Lunden, a rather famous, fun loving young actor who at the start of his epic kayaking trip down the rivers and waterfalls of South America and Mexico had packed a Suisse Army knife, binoculars, three waterproof cameras, six flashlights and the rest of his allotted weight in durable batteries knowing the nights would be dark, and the lodgings primitive. He wanted to read. Julian's only real fear were crocodiles, everyone else on the crew dreaded broken backs, noses, ribs or jungle fever, bad food, lack of booze, and violent natives, all of which had become a reality on different legs of the first part of the trip. In the jungles of South America, they were lost often. It was a great dark adventure that promoted his image as a thrill seeker, and provided a reasonable end to a love affair in which a minor starlet, Laynia, was hinting she might be carrying Julian's child. He didn't believe it. He'd felt infertile his entire life.

There was a moment when his father's scowling face appeared in his mirror, that child of a poor reindeer village who had become a wealthy Norwegian was still alive but able to haunt Julian anyway. The man still cut his own firewood to save money, and might've sold his only son at twelve for not proving useful, if the law had allowed. Anyway, by that time Julian had cleverly escaped to a boarding school far out of his reach, and saved himself. Julian scowled back at the face, comically lifted a handsome brow, as he was known to do in his lighter movies, and tossed out the mirror. No one else was shaving.

At the first airport he'd found a book on knot tying, *Knots for Paddlers*, on a chair. He thought this indicated it was something he would need, strongly, and not coincidentally, so he brought it along, too. It was often boring once settled into camp, and tying different knots with a twenty inch piece of round elastic cord could be spell binding. For some impenetrable reason a thought of his mother entered his mind, Julian took a piece of string, tied a slipknot around the tip of his pinkie, and hung her, dispatching both his parents in under ten minutes. If only it were so easy, he sighed.

"Juli, check out the ass on these Water Logs," Grey Mars turned around and pulled the faded orange trunks tight against his skin. Before they began their trip Mars had shaved his head. Now his hair stood two inches from his head, a soft brush of red bristles all over, like a feathery halo that blazed in the Mexican sunlight. Evidently he'd taken to coloring his hair before the shaving; Julian had always known him as brown headed, with never a hint of the ginger. His usually neutral skin was covered in freckles, his nose now a brilliant slick of red from all the peeling in spite of the nose bridge he secured under his dark sunglasses.

"Why do you always call your swim trunks *Water Logs?*" Julian asked what had become a standard, almost rhetorical question whenever Mars came out in them. When Mars didn't answer because he was busy twisting around to check his own ass, like a dog, Julian said, "Well I can see your glowing white ass through the threads if that's what you are asking."

Mars always laughed like a desperately starved hyena ready to attack his next meal, a sound that always made Julian laugh, too. He didn't know why, but he always appreciated the trigger.

"Juli, you feeling okay these days?"

"Never better, why do you ask?"

"You got this thin blue line around your eyes. Your whites are a little blue, too. After that bang up and those weird native band aids, I worry."

Julian's fingers automatically went to his hairline where he'd suffered a slice from some sort of Amazonia flora or fauna, he wasn't sure and got patched up with a flora salve by a local *curandera*. The pain had vanished immediately, along with the scorching burn on his entire scalp the encounter produced.

"It's healed already." He couldn't find the spot with his fingertips.

"Sure you don't want to see a real doctor? Maybe that plant was infected something."

"I don't need a doctor, Daddy," Julian joked as if his father would have ever raised this level of concern over even a chopped off finger, or several.

"Let me see the skin on your scalp. Your color is off. It isn't some weird make up trick you're using to scare the kids in the village?"

4

"It's called a pueblo down here. My scalp is fine." But his fingers went to it anyway. It felt like it normally did.

"I know you're still brooding over Lana, but I think you've been enjoying this, trip."

"Yes I have," Julian agreed, clamping a hand over his friend's shoulder and squeezing the hard muscle. "And I haven't been brooding over Lana, she was using me to get attention."

"Well that's Hollywood love, my friend," Grey said.

Grey Mars was his assistant, his detail man, financial manager, and agent. Although two men could not be more opposite in looks or personal obsessions, they fell in together anyway and clicked. Both were fit, determined men capable of powering through the turbulent rivers of South America and forging new paths on foot. They weren't in the least bit competitive, more like monkey see, monkey do, which at times had proven itself just as hazardous as any spirited contest. All through the lousy, noisy, stinking Amazon jungle, and its surrounding lesser-cousin jungles they had snapped pictures and taken notes discussing the possibilities for some sort of movie. Everything they viewed was with the stern focused eye of a camera lens, making movies, maybe, was their real binding tie.

"You know I regret we didn't bring anything real to film with. I would have loved to capture Muff stepping off that fall holding his PFD straps like he was bracing his parachute. Feet first, how high was that? Hit the water and popped out like a cork!" Mars went on muttering.

"He's lucky he didn't break a leg, or worse. Jeezus can you imagine the trouble that would've caused everyone," Julian bristled.

"Aw, come on. You can't be the only daredevil. And it wasn't like he was begging for applause. He stepped off the cliff of a waterfall and plunged into the God damn wild water below without any fanfare. That was something. Like he did it for himself."

"Yes, it was unbelievably nuts," he conceded as best he could. It was an incredible plunge off a rather narrow, but high— yes hundreds of feet high-- waterfall. They'd all been gathered at the edge wondering if it would be too dangerous to go off in their kayaks. Their guides insisted it was safe and went to get into their boats to prove it. It was at that point, when it was just the collection of Americans that Muff Head (as they'd all taken to calling him when the wet jungle released his hair into a giant muff) just stepped off without warning, or even a decent war-whoop. Julian had felt upstaged and incredibly envious at the subtle show of superiority over them all.

"Good crew, all around," Mars chuckled.

"Yes it is," Julian easily conceded the point because it was true.

Mars had invited the entire production crew from some sort of movie of the Hercules, or Zeus, or Gladiator type, he'd been recently attached to. Six came along. Julian called them the lights, camera, action crew. All big strong Jews—an oxymoron if you believed the stereotypes-- and the kind of smart men Julian expected to have good ideas when these were called for. They hadn't disappointed him.

Except for the guides, none of them were diehard kayakers, but to a man they all had respectable enough whitewater experience. As teens, they had run the big spring melt whitewater on the tricky rivers of their hometowns, and beyond. Of course they all went anticipating what their challenges would be, but the size of these South American rivers- water turned into thundering liquid roller coasters filled with hungry deadly animals were nothing they could have ever imagined. The assortment of National Geographic films, and YouTube videos they all watched before going did not do it justice. The profound isolation from the rest of the civilized world left them having frequent, if not spare discussions about the primitive death that might be awaiting them.

"Never felt I'd drown on a river."

"Or get eaten by a pack of fish with teeth."

No one mentioned the possibility of larger lizards with teeth. This would have been too much to contemplate.

The roar of the river was relentless and the more they listened the more swallowed by it they felt.

"How would they recover the body?" was asked without specifying whose body.

Someone snorted. "Forget your body. Focus on the soul escaping unharmed. We'll give a huge send-up back home."

"Empty coffin, but we'll make it lavish. Let the loved ones fill it with notes."

Several of them groaned, then they all took another tact, chipping in with:

"Aren't we paying for expert guides? I mean like the very best."

"Isn't this like a tourist industry thing?"

"Only for the very special tourists." Someone else joked.

"This is not Magic Mountain roller coaster rides, boys. We knew what we were getting into before we signed on."

"The guides will mark the spot with crosses, votives, and flowers. No worries," Mars had probably said this, with complete sincerity, like that would be more than enough to commemorate this spoiled man's journey.

This didn't exactly quiet them, though. The guides were natives who knew the river as their playground, they were also religious, and seemed to accept death as only Mesoamericans with that still-not-quite-dry-veneer of Catholicism do.

None had suggested quitting, but they began to put on the river each morning with grim determination, and took off in the afternoons with grateful silence, hearts thumping for hours afterward. Every night they ate and drank like it would be the last. And then they got to the fun sport of shooting off low waterfalls into the churning pillows of water the pour over created. After Muff stepped off the cliff, they began behaving like crazed teens with no sense of their mortality. They brushed their teeth with tequila. Everyone tried to speak Spanish. Julian thought all they needed was a priest, a river baptism, another button of peyote and they'd all go ape shit.

Julian felt proud they had all adapted. Every step of the way they pulled their own weight, ate and drank what was at hand, took their scrapes, bang ups and broken equipment with the kind of deranged joy these kinds of occurrences brought out in adventure seekers. There were no fistfights, really no blaring arguments either. These were men used to working under pressure, and as a team. All in all, Julian found it to be a dream vacation.

"It's a great crew, Mars," Julian repeated, meaning it.

## Chapter Two

Day six of their trip they finally landed on the gentler, calmer, less-dangerously-animal infested states of Mexico, southwest of the Yucatan and thereabouts to be less than precise, but Mars had to jet home almost immediately to see to a business emergency. The trip flattened for Julian; even after only a few hours, he missed him, his only equal in the sense that Mars could always be counted on to tell him the truth. A quality of friendship that kept Julian not just alive, but morally strong, and working as an actor.

Alone at the river's edge Julian leaned inside the kayak to adjust the practically prehistoric foot pegs, and then readjusted the antique backrest before he'd put into the water. They were paddling old model boats now. They'd busted up their good boats on the heinous sections of South American rivers, one they had given to the guides, as a tip with the money tip. The group was now down to the lesser, back up boats, those they could scrounge up in Mexico. These were the old-fashioned roto-molded kayaks, designed before the advent of inflatable Happy Feet, and Sweet Cheeks. The boat was too roomy, and he was having a bit of difficulty finding its fit, but Julian believed that great whitewater kayaking should always come with unexpected challenges. That was the whole point of adventure. Julian sat inside, pulled the spray skirt snugly around the opening, sealing him in, tight as a drum. He got the feel of his paddle, dug into the water for some trial braces, a couple practice rolls, before settling in and joining the group.

The sky was a clean, airy blue and this morning anyway, unusually cloudless. He was last on the water, but as ready to go as the rest of his crew. The current was slow; the eddy they all sat in was almost a pond. The water was clear, wonderfully warm, and tumbling downstream with the relaxed pace of the small Mexican pueblo they were now bunked down in. The Gulf of Mexico was near enough to feel it's feisty, scorching air wafting toward them.

After two miles of rippling wave trains, the roaring of the first waterfall made Julian mentally rub his hands together in glee. In his own boat, he never missed the line, never failed to find that one sweet spot- the slick tongue of water that helped the boat slip over the calamity of turbulent whitewater into the next drop.

The leader lifted his paddle and signaled to eddy out, river right.

"Man that water sounds like its pounding off the ledge," someone shouted excitedly.

"Oh, come on. The current is barely tugging. And it isn't deafening."

They got out to check the falls, visually map the line, watch a couple of the Mexicans go first. Julian estimated twenty feet to the tip of the boulder that was dividing the line into two parts. The Mexicans each took a hard right even though it cost them speed and required a difficult rotation to get into the current proper. They made swift, succinct paddle strokes and held the line, so they must have had their disasters here. Julian liked to watch Pedro paddle in the red boat he prized more than his shoes. The kid attacked the water like it might run out before he could get down the river. As someone in a ridiculously competitive industry, Julian admired ruthless pursuits.

The Mexicans used the shortest paddles he'd ever seen. They slapped the water with flattened blades rather then dig into it, and moved the boat by force of their lower body, which every kayaker did, but he'd never seen a boat maneuvered with the skill and power these diminutive Mexicans used with their abdominals, hips and legs. When one of their crew broke their paddle, they threw them theirs and paddled on with their hands. Their kayaks skimmed the surface of the water like ducks, even when the rest of them were getting buried. Moving toward the falls they slapped their paddles right, left, more right, more left. He could feel the power in each shift of their hips even as he stood on the bank just watching. At the terminal point, to a man they howled some primal yell before going over. It always made Julian feel too uptight; too civilized. Girlish even. He left the terminal edge with his lips sealed shut, afraid the paddle shaft would rear up with the force and break his teeth.

"Landed flat on the hulls," someone reported. The sigh was collective. Everyone knew the pain from the spanked tailbone, a painful current zipping up the spine. They all moved back to their boats, wishing for double mats of silicon pads on their seats.

Going near last, Julian paddled confidently into the strong current, boofed a submerged rock and got knocked a few inches off the very narrow line. Shifting his weight to correct as he swept his paddle, he again veered off the line by a couple of inches, these near-corrections would make all the difference, but then there he was at the lip: he could only stroke hard over the fall, get his paddle shaft away from his teeth. From the angle of his boat, his stern was too high; he knew he was going to pencil straight in. He leaned forward and set up to roll, knowing he was going to hit the water, flip ass over tin cups in the turbulence and get trashed by the pour over. This all came to be.

Upside down and disoriented, a wall of rock prevented him from setting up his onside roll and spooling back to the surface. He banged the edge of his paddle against it hoping the current would pull him out. It didn't. His offside roll caused him to sputter helplessly on the surface sucking air before he let the boat close him back under the water. Six more set up and fails came in rapid succession before he considered punching out and taking a swim to the shore, a tactic he would not give into short of drowning. By stroking with his paddle under water and upside down in his boat, he managed to move out of the hurricane of the pour over, and snap up a roll using the current. The rest of the crew cheered him from the eddy. Applause was something he came to expect. Paddling with bruised dignity towards them, he promised himself to practice his off side roll, one hundred times before he ate again.

Late that afternoon, against the protests of the locals, Julian threw his boat into a small mountaintop lake that seemed to have formed in the basin of an ancient volcano. The water was almost steaming warm. The Mexicans shook their heads gravely.

"*Que haces?*" Julian shouted at them.

"*Esta encantada!*"

"*Embrujada!*"

"*No es seguro. Esta llena con fantasmas!*"

"*No, solamente es veneno,*" another cried, all backing off so it wouldn't damped so much as a toe.

Julian didn't believe it was haunted, filled with ghosts or poison, too many birds were drinking from it. When he paddled out to a deep spot in the crystal clear water, he had to chase the ducks out of his way by swinging at them with his paddle. Just as he'd promised himself he did his off side roll over one hundred times. To spook the Mexicans he took a drink of the water. They lugged the boat and equipment back down the steep mountain in silence, but he knew throughout the night they would be watching him for signs of spirit possession, or at least a bad case of diarrhea, but they were disappointed. His fortitude only stirred more awe in them, and increased their reluctance to hover too near. After that, no Mexican accidentally touched Julian.

Xilitla was a small pueblo that specialized in Mexican soul food that most visitors never experience, a dozen different kinds of chilies, all hot as fire crackers, sauces woven with the magical spices of the local flora. Against the advice of every travel book they collectively brought, they drank homemade *pulque* from the local dirt-floor bar. The thick, almost disgusting cloudy liquor, coupled with a nibble of a touch peyote button did produce hallucinations, which Julian rather enjoyed, he liked surreal events to puncture his so-called real life, and the next morning he awoke bright and energetic, the only one without a brain damaging hangover.

"How are you today Senor?" The cook asked as Julian piled mini-roasted chilies on the fresh chicken mole, beans, eggs, with chopped and steaming *nopalitos*.

"Not as good as this food." Julian spoke a pretty rapid Spanish. In his entire life he didn't think he felt more energetic, or free of inner turmoil, but he didn't like to brag.

A crowd of women and children gathered near his table, later the men sauntered over with their cracked mugs of *cafe con leche*. They used canned condensed milk, a product Julian had also grown up with, on the opposite side of the world. Making a small show if it, he tipped some into his own cup, saluted one and all, and drank up, setting his cup down with a flourish. All eyes watched it rest on the table before turning back to him.

When he moved, they moved, something most people might've found unnerving, but he was used to the locals collecting together and staring at him. Norwegian bleached blonde hair, blue eyes, the squared chin and broad forehead; he often found himself staring at his own image. After all, he was a popular movie star for a reason.

The last few days of their stay, the crew decided they wanted a couple of days rest: abundant resort food, American beer, sleep, a little prowling around the local resorts for gifts for their loved ones who were waiting less than patiently for their safe return back home. There were also some bars with exotic dancing girls they'd heard about. The furry faced beasts all packed with glee. Julian decided this was a perfect opportunity to help the locals with their failing water supply.

A little known fact about Julian Lunden, award willing film actor, was that he studied engineering. In truth is was cursory, and only as his cover for his acting classes to keep his father from bodily removing him from the southern California university he had to fight his way into against his father's wishes. Another little known fact about his country of birth: Norway is the third largest oil exporter on Earth, producing around 3 million barrels of oil per day, and the world's sixth largest producer of natural gas. Thanks to the significant gas reserves in the North Sea. It was the source of the country's wealth and certainly much of his father's, Julian hoped anyway. Naturally, water was much easier to convey through a pipe than oil sucked from the freezing sea. It wasn't filthy dirty or subject to the oddities of chemical reactions, or the explosive emotions of greedy people.

Anyway in just a couple of hours of following the supply lines it was clear that the source of their problems didn't need any kind of engineer to figure out. Most of the pipes were above ground and so full of cracks he guessed they lost eighty percent of the water to the barren ground. Leaks had to be sealed; that seemed pretty straightforward. It took a couple of days to get the new pipe, PVC cement (Mexico sold a shameful cheap lesser version of schedule 40 PVC that wouldn't be used for sprinkler lines in the USA, and instead of sealing the joints together with cement they used old hair blow-dryers to mold the ends together one inside another, a fact that made Julian shake his head in wonder that these people had any water at all.) Julian procured the PVC cement from a hotel construction site, giving a large bribe, and got to work. Water pressure finally became a reality, but he knew it couldn't last for long. These humble people would need a more help, a well and some type of purifier. They needed a hand washing station at the tap, too. He needed to get back to the USA to get the aide of a special interest group interested enough to scare up funding, an expert who spoke Spanish so the people could learn how to repair their own pipes, dig a well, purify the water, wash their hands, keep their animal shit out of the river. Once they got the water flowing in from the river again, they had a small, colorful fiesta. Celebrations are something Mexicans are excellent at. Julian loved the dancing, it seemed to respect and admire their women like nothing else did in this culture.

During these last few days in the pueblo the locals began bringing him cold teas, and other herbal remedies, one shyly suggested the services of the local *curandera*.

"*Por que?*" He asked surprised they thought there was something wrong with him when he never had felt better.

"*Su piel!*" They cried. True Mexicans never point. It is considered the rudest of rude behaviors, so they held out their own arms, pinched their own flesh. They thought his skin was burning, but it wasn't.

"*No quemo!*" Julian told them, holding out an un-sunburned hand to make his point. A real shower would go a long way, he had a thin layer of the grayish river mud coating his skin, but otherwise every muscle in his body hummed with juiced energy.

One baking hot afternoon the lights, camera, action crew returned, revived, with haircuts and cleanly shaved. In fact, it looked as though they'd never been on any type of adventure, which is what Julian supposed they wanted when they greeted their women, no residue of time spent away having fun. Their newly scrubbed appearance made Julian rub at his own furry face, but he decided to shave when he got home. The press would eat it up. After emerging from the van, they came immediately to Julian and for a few minutes seemed to study him. The red head, Dirk or Derek, Julian didn't like the name well enough to stamp it into his thoughts, stepped forward like he had something of importance to tell Julian. Whatever he wanted Julian took some sort of mild offense and stepped away. Derek too stepped back and rubbed the top of his own head as if to tap a thought back inside.

"How's it going?" One of the cameramen asked with an odd uplift in his voice.

"We got the waterline repaired. I'm ready to get home."

"Julian, you need to take a look in the mirror. You look sallow, but like in a blue kind of sallow way," Muff Head (now Shaved Head) finally said.

"Sallow means yellow," Julian informed them.

"Dude, you're blue," Derek stated, taking a stand.

"The pure color of a clear sky," someone else added.

Julian checked himself out in the mirror and was mildly shocked to find that he did, indeed, look blue. Not ready to believe he could be the color of a pale sky he decided to waste some of the newly piped water on a shower and shave. The grayish-blue mud swirled around his feet in the water. He shaved the blonde hair off his face and was startled by how young, and blue tinged he really was. He checked his tongue, it was the usual pink. When he rubbed his flesh it went pink at the touch, but when he let go it took on the blue hue. And then he stopped worrying over it, and finished packing.

While the crew staggered around packing the van in silence, the Mexicans stood in a semi circle clutching their crosses, praying silently. Julian could not exactly read their expression, but he thought it was affection and something else that made his toes tingle like an electrical current ran through them. The Mexicans all waved goodbye with exuberance. Obviously it was a deep relief that they were going, something much more than the generous tips they gave them.

"This was an awesome trip, Julian!" The men all agreed. Julian did too, but he was busy rubbing first the blue spot on his hand and then looking at his face in the rearview mirror. If he put his hand outside the window under the brilliant sun it looked the normal color, but in the van his skin was definitely blue.

By the time he got to the airport he was the pale blue of a robust bloom of an agapanthus. Every inch of his skin, even his ball sack, he had checked in the toilet stall, had changed to this color—blue-- and his eyes, already a stunning azure, became something more crystalline, two diamonds radiating out of his handsome, blue face. In the harsh fluorescent lights of the airport he practically glowed. People stepped aside to let him pass. The security guard leapt away when Julian asked him for gate information.

Luckily, they were leaving at an hour when the airport wasn't crowded. It helped that Mars had prearranged for them to use the VIP facilities. There were fewer than one hundred people in that section, but of those, the tourists, the airport workers, the maintenance people, everyone began talking excitedly as soon as he entered. Julian was used to it. In fact he secretly loved the paparazzi, but he wasn't so dense not to understand the under current: this event with Julian was different. The crowds parted for them, oddly, no one tried to touch him. People loudly commented that this was staged event, someone even called out, "what's the new movie, Julian?" The paparazzi always spoke to him like they were close personal friends passing each other in the neighborhood.

A skinny man with a string mop, stopped to lean on the handle, and watch. A mahogany colored dog wagged its magnificent tail and started to prance over, pulled off by his master and hurried into his cage whining like he was really missing out on the sniff-down of a lifetime. Most everyone recognized Julian and *thank God* thought it was a publicity stunt for a new movie.

A representative of the airline, their escort whispered, "Hey, Mr. Lunden, are you making another Aqua Man movie?"

"Time will tell," one of his crew filled in for him as Julian's thoughts skittered, something that never happened before. His thinking was always anchored tightly to his chosen subject, this scattershot- no orbital--no drunken whirl-- of thoughts scared him. He kept a dignified posture, a casually indulgent smile for the onlookers, but followed his crew like a toddler might keep up with a parent. His knees wobbled, his hands shook.

After a brief, very private phone conservation with Mars, it was decided that Julian's first destination in the U.S. would be a clandestine trip to the best hospital nearest the first American airport they were to land in. Florida. Grey Mars was on his way.

Julian's crew settled into their first class seats laughing with that giddiness that travel usually brings out. They were the only group. The flight attendants were overly solicitous with Julian, like they were almost afraid of him, but no one asked him any questions although one well sculpted male attendant in a ridiculous neck scarf did try giving off a series of raised eyebrows, followed by a conspiratorial eye query, as if Julian was about to confide in a stranger. And he wasn't gay, so there would be no connection there either.

Julian turned to the flight attendant at hand and said, "Would you bring me a *cup* and by cup I mean a generous eight ounces of liquor strong enough to cause tears just by the *smell. And* I need a separate cup filled with crystal clear ice." The ice was to run over his forehead. The cold sometimes helped him to think.

"Right away, sir," the attendant spun around and disappeared behind the magic curtain where all good things awaited.

The lights, camera, action crew got busy adjusting their pillow-y first class seats that relaxed into beds with a touch of a button, settled in their drinks, their trays, their boxes of playing cards, their individual movies, all first class cabin luxuries that Julian provided for them both coming and going, and now regretted it, if only in an almost negligible way. Their fresh haircuts made him angry, he rubbed his fingers through his own long, stringy mop.

As if on cue they all looked at him, removing their ear buds. "You okay Julian?"

"Why the fuck did none of you bother to mention that I was turning blue?" He demanded.

"We didn't try to tell you. We told you. Back at camp, before we left."

That was true, he remembered now, but thought they were razzing him.

"Figured it was some jungle crap."

"It was an epic trip Julian. Relax, they'll get rid of it in an American hospital. You need a course of antibiotics."

"We also thought it looked really, really good on you. We were all just saying how nice you looked blue. How it matches your eyes so well," someone else added. After that the sarcasm fizzled off. They knew better than to let this become a merciless ribbing, as they might have done with each other. The flight attendant brought him a drink on ice. He took it, without correcting his order and sat down. It wasn't going to be nearly strong enough, he could tell by the delicate scent of a wimpy, 80 proof vodka.

"You're gonna be okay, Julian," they all assured him. Julian studied each of them.

"Of all of us, why am I blue?" He asked, rolling a fist under his chin. No one followed up with an answer.

# Chapter Three

The hospital did all manner of tests: mercury poisoning, some kind of clever prank, tattoo gone wrong, some weird accidental skin staining, liver damage, an unheard of case of hereditary *methemoglobinemia* finally making itself known. As each test came back negative and his skin slowly deepened to an even Eton blue, he began to understand its impact. Julian's general health remained robust, his muscles now easily bulked with the lightest bit of weight lifting. Running caused euphoria, but he never tired, sugar tasted like sand. No one could explain what was making him blue.

After all of the testing and to make a long, often incomprehensible story, filled with medical terminology, short, the news was not good. Julian was still blue with no hope of returning to normal, unless it decided to vanish as mysteriously as it had appeared. The color was too dark a blue to really hide with much effect. He decided against make up. Scientists asked permission to map his DNA or genetic sequence, genomes, or something equally microscopic and scientifically perplexing; he'd stopped listening after the bad news: no cure, and left without granting permission for them to use his bodily fluids. Julian could care less if he was any kind of benefit to mankind, at all.

Slowly, and it took months, he began to understand that his career might just be finished. The backlash from the news media was brutal and unrelenting. For a while he attempted a public relations junket: writing a blog about acting and extreme sports, his recent kayaking adventure, and turning blue, even allowing local television news to send their entertainment reporters, but if anything these seemed to make matters worse. He was labeled alternately as being poisoned, diseased, a space alien, or a new breed of man, and not any of it reported in a kind way. Now instead of being described as being ruggedly handsome, he had *cartoonish* good looks. Big, big chuckle. Of course he never heard from Lana and her baby belly again. Outside of Grey Mars's steadfast friendship, people no longer invited him to anything, and he couldn't remember the last time someone (besides Grey) had taken his hand, let alone pecked at his cheeks. Mars was a hugger, but Julian really wasn't, and Mars always respected that. Needless to say, they never kissed cheeks. There was nothing to do but to seek every type of medical treatment to be found on the planet. He went everywhere and tried everything. Nothing changed. Julian remained blue.

The day Grey Mars showed up with a play, and an offer without an audition, Julian almost wept with joy. Shakespeare; Othello with adjustments to make it futuristic-cutting edge. It wasn't until he was in the second week that he'd realized it was meant as a *comedic* parody, of him. Although they couldn't have made it more obvious with the space age costumes and lines like this:

*Her name, that was as fresh*
*As Dian's visage, is now begrimed and blue*
*As mine own face.*

He had been too desperate to believe they wanted him, setting himself up by missing the obvious right there in the script. There was no point in blaming Mars, he was as desperate as Julian to believe, too.

The critics were brutal. There were no Politically Correct standards to hold back their outrage against a newly turned, blue man. They all reported on his blue skin like it was something he was doing on purpose, to get attention by coloring himself like a lizard. Julian went into a blinding depression, a loaded gun at the ready.

One dark morning Mars pounded on his door before letting himself in with his key, took a look around at the garbage can that was now Julian's usually immaculate Hollywood Hills home, and headed right for the bedroom. Julian followed him anxiously ashamed his thoughts could be so easily read. Mars located the gun, removed the clip, and dropped it into his coat pocket like this was a part of his daily routine.

"You know, Chekhov says if a gun shows up in a scene it has to go off at some later scene. Or during the last scene. To paraphrase, one of us is going to get shot," Julian told him.

"This ain't ever gonna be Chekhov's gun. You got any others here?" Mars demanded.

"No, and I don't like losing that gun. It's going to be very hard to replace. Being blue, I can't exactly stroll into a gun shop incognito and buy myself a fancy new Ruger, with matching bullets."

"You don't need a gun, Juli, come on! You need a maid. A team of maids. This place is a dump. It looks like the inside of my car. You know I'm going to have to get a crime scene cleaning crew over and I'm going to tell them to clear out all razor blades, firearms and poisons. Holy Shit, Juli, this is about as scary as you can fucking get. You, my friend, need a shift in perspective, and a psychiatrist. Blue or no blue, this is beyond wallowing." He was patting his pocket, where the impotent gun now lay, a gesture that Julian read as Mars ensuring it would not slip out on its own and do its dirty work, as scripted by important classic literature.

Julian leaned his full weight against the huge picture window in his bedroom. "You know I live on a cliff," he said drily.

Mars turned to him, and said quietly, "Pack up Juli. I found an Indian shaman who wants to see you. Says he knows of blue men from some cave paintings and such. Maybe he has some wisdom for you."

"Indian with a turban or a feathers headband?"

"American Indian. The real deal. He says he can help. Try not to offend him with your Norwegian sense of everyone should be white, Norwegian, and male."

"I'm an American. I chose to become one. And I have no accent in my English or prejudice in my soul."

"Pack for the desert which is both hot and cold now," commanded Mars, already fiddling with his phone, ordering up a team of special housemaids with experience for rooting out and dispensing with any dangerous objects secreted in a home.

Julian found the high Arizona desert enchanting. They hadn't gone to the Navajo Reservation as he had believed they would, instead, they drove for nine hours to Sedona, Arizona. Realistic movie sets aside, he'd never been to a real desert before and had not even seen pictures of a red earth desert either. It was a wonderland, in the way he imagined a distant planet would look. Standing between two ancient red rock formations he almost forgot he was blue. And then a bug hit his hand and he flinched, when he lifted it up to check for damage the color startled him. Still blue. Always blue.

"I glow brighter against this red earth," Julian said turning his hand against the red rock.

"Put your hand away then. Look around. This is true natural beauty. Someone said that God created the Grand Canyon, but he lives in Sedona."

"Supposing there is anything like one god, why would he settle in one place? Or one universe for that matter?"

"It's just a way of saying how cool this place is, Juli. Breathe it in."

"I prefer godless places," Julian said. "Less to fear."

"It's snowing!" Mars cried, like he's just discovered gold.

A few flakes of white settled on their shoulders. There were white caps on the distant, ragged mountains. The surprisingly lush greenery was glistening with a light dusting of white. Julian bent down to see if it was really cold enough to be considered snow.

"I suppose this is snow," Julian used the term snow loosely. Snow to him buried things in cold miserable white, it was mystical, it maimed and killed if you were careless with it. And there were many types.

"It's good, right?" Mars said.

"It's so good," Julian replied sincerely. The cool, clean air was such a relief he could not inhale deeply enough. Mars started sucking it in, too. They stood like that side by side, taking it all in.

It was April, and had been one hundred degrees in Phoenix when they'd stopped to buy gas, at midnight. Two hours north and it was like they entered another planet. Without meaning to, Julian calculated that fifteen months had passed since he first turned blue. The two men started on a narrow path together. Only Grey Mars knew where they were headed, but he seemed reluctant to lead.

"I didn't realize there were so many plants in a desert," Julian remarked. "And that it could smell so good. I can't wait to get in a good hike. I haven't really exercised in months."

"I'll rent us mountain bikes. They got great trails here. You're going to love it. Excellent to get out of stinking Hollywood for a change. I don't think they have air pollution here at all. It almost hurts to breathe," Mars chuckled happily breathing in the rich air with another exaggerated sucking in. Julian was never glad to leave Los Angeles. He loved the Hollywood box, and wished he could crawl back in it and revert to his thoughtless, shallow, real self with his mob of fans, the parties, and his natural, white, clear Norwegian skin. He held a blue hand up to the clear blue sky and watched it blend in, like camouflage. From there his thoughts tumbled, he wondered what it would be like to die from carbon monoxide poisoning. A gentle death, so easily arranged. Mars would never forgive himself, Julian thought sadly. This was the only thing that would stop him.

"This way. Let's get this over with," Mars announced, taking longer, confident strides now, leading the way.

A few minutes later they were sitting in a nicely built lodge, small, but the flood of natural light through the slit windows in each of its six corners, made it feel almost like they were sitting outdoors. The architect took inspiration from the Indian teepees of bad Hollywood movies, except he used concrete and there was no smoke hole at the top, no stove of any kind. The thick rug smelled recently vacuumed. The Shaman, was not as enchanting as the place: he had incredible, nose-punching, eye-watering body odor, a kind of pungent forest-on-fire smell, and also he had a funny way of talking. Not accented or Hollywood Indian, but some kind of speech impediment, like his tongue was too thick for his mouth. He frequently spit when he spoke. They sat on the rug in a knees-all-around-circle with both Mars and Julian leaning back to keep out of the spittle spray. In the middle of their small circle was an assortment of stones the Indian kept picking up, shaking in his hand and dropping, like dice, after which he began rearranging. Julian wasn't sure if he was playing some Indian version of solitaire or divining something about the two of them. Or if he was stoned and playing with some very pretty, colored stones.

"You feel blue, but that ith all an illusion."

"I *feel* blue? I *am* fuc---"

Mars elbowed Julian, crushing his eyebrows together as he pulled a face. Julian folded his blue hands into his lap making a mental note to order more blue clothes, end the contrast here and now; stop thinking he may chop his hands off to avoid seeing them. He couldn't wear gloves, he was good with his hands, and that would be a coward's act. Too vain. Getting blue clothes would take less than a week. Thank the gods for the Internet; his thoughts ran in a line.

The Shaman said a bunch of other things Julian could hardly absorb. If everyone here thought he would eventually accept being blue, they were insane, but he did agree about true visions and false realities. And then it occurred to him that Grey Mars was listening and interacting with the spiritual guide with better than polite attention. He was there to learn something. It was the first time in months that it occurred to Julian that his friend was in some way, suffering the ill effects of life, in silence. Out of deference of Julian's blue skin. Mars always chose bad women, so it followed.

"Are you ready to ethperienth--"

Mars assured the Shaman that they were ready to experience. The man spoke some more garbled words. Julian got: interconnectedneth, healing, unknown god, ancesthors, clouths, tholy breaths, thair.

The Shaman didn't call himself that; his name was Malcolm. Julian restrained himself from pointing out to Mars that the name was from Shakespeare, the play Macbeth at that, so Scottish *and* a murderer, or at the very least someone who might want to get even with all the white men who took a flame thrower to his relatives.

"Is this Indian drunk or Scottish?" Julian whispered when the Shaman left to get more magical things for a more complete revelation, if Julian understood him correctly.

"Stop it. You know it's a speech impediment," Mars said patiently settling into his cross-legged posture, a relaxed hand on each knee, almost a yoga pose. The most serene he had ever seen Mars. "He's an American Indian. Pure blood," Mars finished up with.

"He looks garden variety European mix up to me. Italian, Greek, even French."

"All humans originate from Africa." Mars rejoined, the equivalent to a mother's: *I said enough!*

"Did he say we were going to dance praise to an unknown creator?" Julian said, trying to go along.

"The unknown god and the healing power within us all. Try to open your mind and listen to what he has to say."

"Pardon?" Julian teased, cupping his ear.

"Don't piss me off, Juli. As you can see, I'm taking this seriously."

"So just why are you here?" Julian asked now that he had confirmation by his flat-face expression that this was Mars's appointment and he had, probably at the last minute, decided he'd best drag Julian along rather than having to return to find his pitiful blue, dead body to deal with. Tears pooled in the inside corners of his eyes, the sure sign of the pathetic, but genuine sorrow that he had left Mars without his friendship.

"Are you sick?" Julian asked, worried.

Mars shook Julian's knee. "No! I'm not dying or anything dramatic. I'm bordering on impotent. I'm healthy. I love my wife, and I desire her, but I have never had that real drive for sex. Never got into porno. Took the gay test in college: nothing. Now that almost killed me, at that age I should've been able to hump anything, like all my roommates were doing, but no. Feels like my joystick is stuck in neutral. I'm sure it's the reason I'm so focused. My thoughts just don't naturally pull to my dick. And sure I can take the blue V pills, but I'd like to have a natural sex drive, like every other man in America."

This took a few moments to sink in. First because he had attended UCLA with Grey Mars, that was where they met as freshmen, and this is the first he had heard of the "gay test" sex event. Julian was thinking back over those years, well, there were lots of things they did differently.

Julian clapped a hand over his friend's shoulder. "I'll behave. And Grey, if every other man had reliable boners, why is there such a drug as Viagra? Never mind. We can pick this experience apart on the way home."

"There you go," Mars said, already getting fidgety. He stayed cross-legged, but his fingers were searching his pockets bring out a pen. While Mars used his pen to work a tiny hole in his sock large enough to poke his toe out of it, Julian regarded his friend, wondering if this was their real binding tie; the secret, shameful lack of the all-defining, all-powering, urgent male sex drive. Maybe they were ambitious instead, or maybe because of it. Julian wasn't neutral about sex, he enjoyed it with women once they got it started, but he didn't spend any time pursuing *kvinnelige kjønnsorganer*. Women used to come to him, and he enjoyed dating them, but never went at collecting them like, well Mars did. Julian had spent most of his free time working on investments, and

24

philanthropy, albeit privately, as it should be done. This was the first moment that Julian thought he might adjust to being blue after all. There must be other work for a man as ambitious as himself.

When Malcolm returned he was carrying some sort of a leather box with what sounded like several glass bottles rattling inside. Julian yawned, wanted badly to think of a way out of there without betraying Mars.

Stepping in a few minutes after Malcolm was a woman with dark hair that stopped below her knees. It stayed behind her back so it took Julian a few seconds to realize it was hair and not part of her outfit, which was just as dark.

"I'm Talia, Malcolm's friend. Blue Man, if you will come with me," she nodded at Julian. Being called Blue Man to his face surprised him so well he stood and followed her without even making eye contact with Grey Mars. Outside they walked to a narrow path and began a steady, but gentle ascent.

"I thought we would take a hike. Just stay on the trail so we don't break the crust on the pristine soil that surrounds it. It's an entire ecosystem in that crust," Talia whispered like she was afraid of waking the sprites. Being Norwegian, Julian understood this type of reverence, and kept his feet on the narrow path.

"Why are we going to hike?" Julian asked, easing off of his pace.

"To begin to explore your spiritual plan."

"Why would I want to do that?"

"We don't have to. I won't presume. It's your reality."

"How old are you?" Julian asked.

"How old are you?"

"Twenty-five," Julian lied. He was thirty-two, but didn't care to admit it to her. Talia started walking faster so he did, too.

At some sort of crossroads of narrow trails, Talia stopped and turned to him.

"You have an old way about you. You seem ancient. But you look young, like a teenager by modern standards, but you talk and act like you are maybe forty, maybe sixty, or even one hundred. Well, too many people think we have to live by a calendar."

Julian suddenly longed for a big drink of Sierra Silver Tequila. He'd take it straight out of a bottle that had sat in a hot car for hours. Checking his watch required looking at his blue hands, but he did it any way.

"Where are we going?" He asked, measuring the time.

"I'm going to take you to this special place. It has petroglyphs – yellow, red and blue people painted on the walls. Handprints maybe of your ancient ancestors?"

Julian laughed. "My ancient ancestors are from the far, far north, the frozen hinterland, I'm afraid. They would never have come here. We're too far from the ocean."

"Where?"

"Norway."

"Norway? Are there other blue people there?"

"No, just the water and icebergs," Julian said, stopping. They were on a ridge. The whole valley stretched below. Brick red and green dotted Sedona now seemed to go on as far as the eye could see, yet he knew just a few miles in each direction, lay normal gray desert, dull and endless with gigantic saguaro cactus. And as all the brochures promised there were dozens of red rock formations, pinnacles of wonder, the jagged leavings of ancient mountains washed away by some corrosive ancient sea, the thicker, smoother bases also dotted in green. *Buy books on prehistoric earth*, he jotted the reminder on nothing but his own thoughts.

The town itself was larger than Julian had thought. The hotel was within walking distance. He could see the roof and grounds, the golf course with those infernal lazy-man's carts. The room, a luxury suite, had a stocked bar, ice, a fridge, room service, a private patio, and an enormous television. Julian had brought along more books to read than underwear. The key card was in his wallet.

Being alone just then scared him. Leaving felt disloyal to Grey Mars who was fighting harder for Julian's life than he was.

"Vikings," he said. "My ancient people were Vikings. I think they used to paint their faces blue before war or mating, or something. Mainly I grew up with stories of the enchanted forest creatures, more ancient than Vikings."

"Vikings? You know, some people think they came here!"

"Here? No. Maybe Canada or New England or the Eastern Seaboard." He wanted to ask Talia if she'd ever looked at a map,

26

but didn't. Julian looked around to see if Grey Mars was anywhere near enough to witness his self-restraint. Still uncertain of what he wanted to do, he stared straight ahead, thinking of the sound of a tumbling river, the waterfalls. What had happened to him in those jungles? This place was just as ancient, just as strange. Should he be afraid now?

"Do you have any questions for me?" She asked. Her voice was lovely. Julian bet she could sing in perfect pitch.

"What's that formation down there called? It appears bigger than the rest," he said just to be polite.

"That's an important cosmic energy field. The colloquial name is Capitol Butte. Some New Age Believers believe there's a gigantic reservoir of crystals inside, and others believe there's a lost city in there."

"What do you believe?" Julian asked intrigued that anyone who knew anything about planet Earth in the modern age could choose either hypothesis? And he used the term loosely.

"Any belief worth having must first, survive doubt. I haven't come to it yet. Is it possible for you to put yourself in my hands for about two hours by your sense of time?" She asked.

"Sure, of course," Julian said with only a hint of sarcasm. They walked in single file on a softly scraped trail of chalky, red earth. Moving over the worn surface was gratifying in its silence. Wild, thick forests of Ponderosa pine grew in the high mountains. The land was breathtaking in its way.

Julian pitied this place because he was certain one day soon, rich people would obliterate what millions of years of water and soil erosion and whatever else caused the formation of these majestic monolithic shapes, the narrow, deep canyons surrounded by arches, buttes and cliffs. In some pamphlet he'd picked up in the hotel room he'd read that iron oxide flowing in the erosive, primordial waters left the warm shades of red as it washed over and through porous sandstone. Julian again thought: order books on geology and paleontology, you don't know anything about the real earth and what lies within.

"I come meditate here almost every day," she was still whispering. Julian kept moving in step with her.

"Here it is!" Talia clapped her hands at the entrance of a cave like she was surprised she found it. Julian hesitated, uncertain if he wanted to step further. Since childhood, caves had a way of putting Julian into strange fugues. Talia went and he followed.

"Look up! Do you see the blue people?"

The figures on the surface of the rocks did look as if it had been painted a deep blue, but nothing like his new color, or even the color of the sky that surrounded it. Some images were scraped into it, and the handprints were primitive, veined like these walls. The impulse to trace his finger over the spiraling shield of the primitive warrior drew him closer. The images looked deceptively near, but the closer he got, the higher they became. He could not touch them without a very tall ladder. Julian held his hand against the cold stone that formed part of the walls studying the primitive rock etchings, his eye finally following the line that lead to the opening in the ceiling, the sunlight path to the boundless heavens. If he had a kayak he would paddle up that liquid gold and disappear into the sun. He held another hand up toward the warrior and his clump of meandering animals feeling that someday, in some distant future, it was possible that he too would be honored as one of the progenitors of all that survived after him, if he could find a way to emerge into the next modern world as this warrior had. Julian always believed he would achieve this through film.

"Yoohoo!" The voice of his mother radiated to him from the dark inside of the cave, as Julian was stepping out of the forest, before dusk. From the door of their yellow barn, his mother waved. Snow on the ground. Thick yellow braid, woven with brilliant strands of color that flowed down her shoulder to her knee. Please, please let me have waved back that time, he thought. Just once, wave back to your mother, hateful, stubborn Julian. This time his tears stung, like fire. He clapped a hand over both eyes, mopping off the moisture.

Then a human hand was on his arm, he looked at it, normal flesh on his blue flesh, slender fingers, symmetric nail tips. Some kind of static electricity zipped through them.

"Wow, did you feel that energy?" Talia asked.

"No," Julian lied, freeing himself of her by simply lowering his arm.

Talia's hand hovered, "Did it hurt you?"

He checked the spot where she'd place her hand to see what would become of his skin now. She looked, too. It was still blue, that smooth, never-fading blue.

"I'm okay," he told her walking out of the cave. Once outside in the open air, he could breathe normally.

"This is an interesting place," Julian said once he felt fully back in his own body, he bounced on the balls of his feet, testing for his full weight.

"This is the land of the true probearers," Talia said. "The *Sinagua*." She pronounced like *sing-waw-waw*, using the cadence of some old Hollywood movie drumbeat of some made up tribal dance. She followed this by whispering, "No one knows what happened to them."

He decided to skip the *un*word, *probearers* and leap onto the other, more offensive (to him), *sin agua*.

"*Sin agua*," he said quietly. "That is two words. Together they mean without water in Spanish. Maybe there was a quarrel, which is what usually ends a group. Maybe white man's disease eventually reached them by wild pigs. But they had their own name before the Spanish opened the death door on the Americas, and it wasn't Sin Agua."

"What?" She said, moving inside her own hair, which fell over both shoulders sheltering herself from him, he supposed, a trick Julian would sorely love to have. The idea was reluctantly discarded; he could not wear a cape. His hair might grow long, his mother's grew almost to her ankles. It occurred to Julian turning blue might have worked better had he been female, but it was just another ridiculous, fleeting thought.

"I don't think it was meant to insult them," Talia said gently.

"It isn't an Indian word, but somehow it stuck, as one, didn't it?" Julian said trying to graciously bow out of being such a big, blue asshole.

"I'm sorry for sounding like such an ass---"

"Let's go back hand-in-hand," Talia laughed, taking his hand in hers. The gesture, the natural reaching to him and weaving of her fingers into his, the human touch, astonished Julian and he could not speak again until she let it go.

They ended up at what Julian would describe as a luxury cabin, built under a series of dome shaped roofs, the color of the iron-rich earth that surrounded it. Inside this cabin were over stuffed sofas and chairs, a fireplace in the center that vented out of the roof. The pillow, and ceramics were the usual geometric American Indian patterns in turquoise, red, green and black. Julian was surprised that he didn't find it appalling. Talia got it started, a clean burning gas flame that felt oddly comforting to Julian.

"How about we try a small cup of peyote tea. Just enough to calm you. This is meant to provide a pathway to your vision. Let you think about new things, in laymom's terms."

Julian badly wanted to correct the word *laymom's*, but he only nodded. There was strong appeal to thinking about something else, even in those misstated terms. He told her he'd like the peyote. Once he agreed she smiled and said, "give me a few minutes. Settle in, the bathroom is that purple door, the yellow door is the kitchen, where I'm going, and that open door over there, which is green, leads to the art studio."

Julian settled into a thickly padded chair and waited. She emerged, as promised, in a few minutes bearing a tray of two ceramic bowls.

"You might feel sick to your stomach before it starts to work. It isn't very strong though. More like a suggestion. Sip it slowly," Talia cautioned, drinking first. They each held exquisitely hand made ceramic mugs. He made a point of not asking about them, although he wanted to know if she had shaped them.

"You hate being blue," she said.

"The skin color of villains," Julian replied, drinking it down in one gulp. "If you're into movies."

"I'm not. Julian, I know you are going through a tough time, but life is like a coin. You can spend it any way you wish, but you only spend it once. Come on, let's paint color into our souls," Talia said. "Malcolm called you father. Do you have many children?" Talia asked.

"No!" Julian laughed; it felt unnatural. He supposed the peyote was working. And then he almost asked her for more.

"Maybe he meant as in the original man with children to follow. Like the Adam, in your religion."

"I'm more likely to grow wings and fly," Julian asked. "And which religion do you imagine I follow? I'm an atheist. Adam and Eve are images from great works of art and nothing more."

"The miracle is not to fly in the air, or to walk on the water, but to walk on the earth," she responded.

Julian thought for a moment before saying, "Life's but a walking shadow, a poor player that struts and frets his hour upon the stage and then is heard no more: it is a tale told by an idiot, full of sound and fury, signifying nothing."

"Are you making fun of me?" she laughed.

"No, that's what William Shakespeare wrote about life. Macbeth Act 5, Scene 5," Julian said seriously.

"Come with me."

Talia lead him to another room where there were actual paintings on the floor, but none on the walls. It smelled of oil paint and something else he could not define in his haze. He was relieved to see a bookcase full of books. On the wall a paper scroll read, *Like the moon, come out from behind the clouds! Shine... Meditate. Live purely. Be quiet. Do your work with mastery. Buddha*

Julian could often approve of Buddha, although many quotes attributed to him were false, he supposed they, at least, kept people thinking about kindness towards all. He wasn't sure if the quote on this particular poster was true Buddha, but there were dozens of signatures in the margins, in many styles, and types of ink, he supposed this was some sort of pledge to a doctrine the people of this commune had signed before hanging it, but he didn't ask her.

"We'll paint sitting on the floor, like this," she folded her legs under her, and settled in front of an expanse of white. Her body was toned, when she moved her muscles separated and showed how they worked to move her bones. Her face was not conventionally beautiful, but she was not ordinary looking and certainly not hideous. No make up, no implanted cheekbones, no surgically dimpled chin or artificially inflated lips, though hers were very full. Her smile was too large and her teeth were the natural yellow teeth were supposed to be, and also crooked. Her face was beautifully angled, but yet rather harsh plains, the cut and color of a Pacific Islander ancestry, to his mind. The signs of aging, the small wrinkles around her mouth and eyes were sexy—he guessed her to be about forty years old. After hours of hair and make up and the boost of perfect lighting, she could be a force on camera.

"Now I am going to mix a blue to match your skin and paint you. I'd like to capture this moment in time, to name it, and thereby free you to become."

The color was accurate, but she rendered Julian in a few flat, curved lines. This unaccountably delighted him. His heart seemed to swell with genuine affection for her honesty.

"I think I'm stoned on peyote," He said, making her laugh.

"Life is slippery. Here, take my hand," she said, turning her bold face up to him. He kneeled next to her, mixed a color to match her skin tone and painted her symbolically, too: a broad round double "u" with dots in the middle. "That's nice," she said. "A joy shared is a joy doubled, isn't it? Like my breasts there. You captured them well, loops with dots." And then she laughed very hard, her head tipped backwards showing her long, neck. How easy it would be for a terrible stranger to wrap his hand around that silken neck and squeeze. She looked heartbreakingly vulnerable. Julian wondered how long she would live given her open naïveté towards men.

Maybe sensing his shift in mood, Talia started giving Julian a gentle massage through his shirt, creating heat on his cold skin. They quickly went from moving creamy colors onto some kind of smooth white board to being locked together on the floor kissing.

"We have a live-and-let-live community. They would welcome you as a messenger from the unknown future," she whispered. "Do you have a lover?"

Julian shook his head. She was undressing him, and he was waiting to see how he would feel about being blue and naked in front of a woman. The sensation of her gentle feminine hand on his skin stupefied him. It had been so long since a woman had wanted to run her hands over his body he thought he would give her—in that moment—anything she asked him for.

"Life without love is like a tree without blossoms or fruit. Lay right on top of my back, cup my breasts and roll me over when you are ready to take me."

The sex was not sex; it was setting free of so many pent up feelings that Julian could not stop. Julian had never been sex-obsessed, he never watched porno, never masturbated, never had one night stands. Every orgasm was a force pulled from his body, leaving him stunned, and completely satisfied. They made love until she closed her legs, suggested a break. After that they drank more peyote, and warm homemade beer, rolled out a large sheet of unprepared canvas, dropped paint on it and fell back into each other's bodies. He was certain he could never return to his old life in Hollywood when there was this paradise to be had, every day of his life. He could be regarded as a demigod, a status not as good as being a famous actor, but better than where he was now, suicidal, alien blue man freak of nature. They made love rolling in the paint, the only lubricant. Her color, his, the earth. He never wanted it to end.

"Then don't go," Talia whispered when he said this out loud.

"Maybe I won't," he answered, running his fingers through her long, silky hair, studying the tips.

But when Grey had come to collect him, Julian went.

"I think I might be in love for the first time in my life," he told Grey Mars later that night when they were back at the hotel to shower and change.

"You aren't in love, you're stoned. Aw, this whole thing was a bust," Mars whispered into his knuckle.

"They have this community up here. Talia thinks I would be accepted, even appreciated, as a blue man. I could just be myself here." He poured a glass of vodka on tinkling, crystal clear ice. It was a work of art, this liquid in this glass, he thought. In his home was a glass sculpture made from lightning striking the beach sand.

"We're getting the fuck out of here," Mars said. "This place is like the goddamn soft underbelly of Holly*weird*-cum-desert-spa-awakening-experience-for-five thousand-dollars-a-day-please."

"I don't understand," Julian said drinking down the welcome fire of the vodka.

"You will after you sleep it off."

They drove home that night, with Julian taking over the wheel as soon as he woke up sober and yet somehow not as discouraged as Mars. He enjoyed the feeling of powering Mars's muscle car down the virtually empty freeway. His thoughts on fucking Talia over and over made him happy. It had been good. Soon, the sunlight began to open the world, a bomb of renewal in this barren land. Julian drove down the empty freeway going one hundred miles per hour. In the barren desert of California there were strange forests of huge manmade windmills. Some were turning. Behind them, somewhere in a land Julian could no longer comprehend, a canvas with smears of paint, his cum, Talia's body heat was drying; stamping down that fleeting moment when he felt real again. He might have even put his signature on it. Now it all seemed like they were leaving a movie wrap party.

"Don't speed through this part of the desert. Listen, when we get home I'm gonna crash in your spare. The wife isn't expecting me home for a few days. If I show up early she'll think I'm not giving this one hundred percent. I'm gonna need time to get the Viagra, too. I need my heart checked first. I have arrhythmia."

"You didn't like Talia at all?"

"Gold digger. She's got something like five kids! She seems to view herself as the original modern Eve, or some bullshit. Did you use a condom? If not, I'm sure you just put a blue kid in there."

"Jesus! Christ! Don't say that," Julian laughed. "She didn't have a single stretch mark." Julian was almost certain they used condoms every time.

"You know sometimes you talk like a woman," Mars said.

Julian laughed. "So what pissed you off?"

"They wanted money to build their artist colony. Felt like a scam."

"Sounded like you just said ant colony. I think my brain is still scrambled. Maybe I'd fit in there. I liked the way she always talked in bumper stickers. Seemed like it would make communication so easy having everything all clipped into short clichés ready to go. I have memorized hundreds of lines. I'd never have to think again."

"You belong to something much larger," Mars said seriously. "It just hasn't appeared what that is yet. So just be patient for once in your life."

34

"You really believe that?" Julian asked.

"Yes, I do."

"And her art, did you see any of it? I think I was impressed." Julian did not mention the sex canvas that she promised to send him once it dried. He decided not to tell Mars.

"That crap? Believe me, if you'd seen it sober, you'd have jumped out of your skin."

"Now that is the miracle I was hoping would happen back there."

"Be patient. You look good blue. People will start to see it," said Mars.

"You know, Grey, sometimes you talk just like a woman. And you are often the most impatient man I have ever known."

That night with Grey Mars snoring loudly in the spare bedroom, Julian stood in the doorway watching his friend, his only brother, really, more important to him than his own father. Mars had told him that he knew his wife slept around, but he pretended he didn't know because he couldn't satisfy her. He wanted her to be happy. It occurred to him that Mars, a fixer of problems, was probably trying to find a way to make him happy, too. Julian wished Mars would find his own happy. Happiness wasn't something Julian ever expected even before he was blue. That was nothing he was raised to ever expect, in that way he was not American, and never would be. No, what he wanted was something more like dull peace, and maybe something to leave on the planet besides the stain of his weird color change.

Satisfied that Mars was sleeping peacefully, Julian went to his own room and checked his email, pleased to find a message from Talia. After he deleted it, he heated the cup of the peyote tea he'd brought back with him in his thermos and drank it down ready to relive that experience one more time. Alone, through only the filter of his warped, Blue Man's mind.

# Chapter Four

The living room of Julian's house was mainly large windows. Many had accused it of looking like a new car showroom, rather than a house. He used to love how he could look out over the canyon on one side and, over the city on the other, and when the haze was gone he could see all the way to the ocean. Littering the floor were pages from The L.A. Gossip, with pictures of Julian in Sedona, his terrible skin glowing against the red earth. Talia was caught with that cape of hair blowing around Julian. She was beautiful, why had he been so critical? He wondered sadly. There were many things he could learn from a woman like her. He also thought he needed to start lifting weights again, his once perfectly tailored clothes hung on him.

Mars thought it was a good sign that they were following him, but Julian needed work, not exposure, and nothing ever came of the photos. Outside the trees were blowing. Julian adored the scorching, dusty San Fernando winds. He opened some windows to air his place, kicking books, cans of food, vases and valuable art sculptures out of the way. The gardeners showed up, turned on the water, a sound from the small bib outside that reverberated through the entire house. Julian looked around for the place he would burrow into.

The sofa got tipped onto its back at some point in the night when Julian was in his now regular drunken uproar. He went to get his bedspread, a *Luc Pilon-Tupin*; the spread had cost over ten thousand dollars. By throwing it over the tipped sofa he made a cave. To hide from the gardeners' noise he crawled inside rolling as far into the merging edges as he could, thinking how the room looked less bleak now, and the sofa back with its hard curve was more comfortable than the seat. Before he could settle into his usual morose thoughts the gardener knocked on the window, one of the problems with having so many of them; he did actually live in a glass house.

"Senor Azul, you got some big delivery onto the driveway!" They had all called him Mr. Blue immediately, like Talia had. He couldn't ignore them.

"Leave it, I'll be there in a minute."

"We're putting it into the garage," the voice called back. The sound of the lawn mower starting vibrated over all others. The pool was actually in the front yard, and the only area with grass so they were just starting. Julian climbed out of his cave, went into the garage to find the orange kayak sitting next to his shining, sports car. He pulled it to his shoulder, took it into his living room, set it down and got inside. It still smelled of the river, he closed his eyes, laid back into a cloudy mist.

Julian, Muff Head, Mars, Brad, and the rest of the crew stood on the lip of the mountain where the waterfall thundered down into the valley. Down below, on a protruding pair of rocks— a formation that looked like an open scissor just waiting to cleave anything that landed in it—was Brad's bright green kayak, tightly wedged. Luckily Brad had punched out before the boat got swept over the fall, landing into the pin.

They were well into hour three trying to get it unpinned. Everyone was muddy, soggy and hungry. For comic relief, Julian's was reading rescue directions from the book he'd found, *Knots For Paddlers.*

"According to Mr. Charlie Walbridge, what we need here is a hauling line. Remember to always wear your PFD and helmet, as a safety precaution. Now what we need do is get a line on the boat and have a group of people on the shore--" This was meant as a joke, there was no shore anywhere near the boat. Earlier they had used the book to lower their kayaks into the pool under the fall. Next, they tried to rig up something from their kayaks, but it had just left them all spinning like a raft of rubber ducks in a wildly swirling pond. The water moved like the flush of the world's most powerful toilet, except it all smelled nice.

"Oh fuck it, leave it. None of us are going to die over a God damn plastic toy."

"Let's go then. It's time for eats and booze!"

Everyone seconded this.

Back at the camp, they were all sitting around the table chowing down a small mountain of spicy food and icy beer, having a raucous post mortem over the day on the river, when one of the Mexican guides came up to them.

"The boat is still stuck," he informed them all. They drunkenly cheered his power of observation, with a loud "Ole!".

The nice things about the crew of Mexicans is most had spent many years in the United States so they had good English.

"Will you abandon it or try again tomorrow to get it out?"

"Screw it. The river can have it. We still got spare boats. Sit down. Have a beer." Mars cried happily.

"Are you truly giving it up?" The guide asked again.

Julian stood up. "You can have it." He told him. "No gringo here is going to die getting it," Julian declared. Everyone seconded it.

Someone cracked another beer, it took that long for it to occur to them that the natives were going to extract that impossibly pinned boat from the roaring river. They knocked the chairs over to run after them and witness the impossible acrobatic feats of daring they were certain were about to happen. No one doubted they'd get that boat. And that there would be blood.

Watching the natives unpin the boat was better than any Sky, Fire, or Snake Dance they'd seen so far. There was bleeding, whooping, but no one died. Also, they were far more ingenious than they had ever been given credit. It took them an hour to get it free, using a Tarzan move they wished they'd caught on film.

"Do you think that could be recreated?" Someone asked.

"Why do we always think we are smarter than these guys?" Someone else asked.

"Under our leftist masks we are still really elitist American bigots without a fucking clue."

They all nodded solemnly.

The guide tried four or five times to give the boat back and when Julian insisted it was his for keeps, he'd earned it, the kid had him sign off a receipt he'd brought with him written neatly in English. This made the entire crew break down in hysterical laughter, but this was silent laugh, shared collectively through the exchange of twitching eyeballs as they all signed off the boat, swigging beer.

Inside the boat, inside his living room, Julian began drifting into sleep. He'd taken to tranquilizers now that the gun was gone; he needed to stop longing for its company. Never before in his life had he understood this hopeless, desiccating affect of depression. The pills began to drag him off. Talia's voice came to him, "Life is slippery, take my hand." She sounded like she was there, next to him. Julian put his hand out, clutched air.

The ringing phone jangled Julian awake. The worst part of coming out of any stupor–always-- was realizing all over again that his skin was blue. Still, he answered the phone without dwelling, a step-up from not ever answering the phone except for a call from Grey Mars, or the grocery delivery driver.

"Hello," Julian said cautiously changing his voice because he didn't recognize the number on the caller i.d.

At first the mad jangle of the foreign language baffled him. It had been so long since he'd heard fluent Norwegian. And then he did recognize who it was and didn't want to understand what was being said, and then he realized *resistance was futile*, was more than just a line from a famous movie, and let it in.

*"Hei far dette er din sønn, Julian."* Hello, Father this is *your son, Julian.* Speaking Norwegian again was like trying to get hot sour grapes out of his mouth. But it also made him nostalgic in the truest sense for he could never recall any part of his wretched home that he could possibly miss.

"Someone showed me a magazine story about your troubles." His father said like he wouldn't believe anything that was written. Julian had to dig deep for sufficient Norwegian language to explain his blue skin while trying to sound like he was not at all affected by it. The conversation never improved after that, but Julian never expected it would go well. His father commanded him, he agreed. He hung up, resigned.

And then, as always, like he knew everything before it happened, Grey Mars called. "Juli, what's up?"

"My father called. I have to go see him in Norway. Actually, a little worse, Svalbard."

"Don't they breed the polar bears there?"

Julian always appreciated how well Grey Mars knew world geography.

"Is there anyway you can come along?" Julian asked.

"As a matter of fact, I'm going that way anyway on a project. To England. I'll get you there and back though. Can't wait to meet your old man."

"I'll pay," Julian said.

"Nawp. I can expense it. And listen Juli, we need to have that serious talk about your finances."

Julian already knew what was going to be said; he was going broke. He had lots of money, but it wouldn't last a lifetime. It was basic math. He needed to earn an income, and reduce his cost of living.

# Chapter Five

SNOW CAVES, his father eats a fresh lemon whole and snaps apples in half for the rest of them to enjoy.

Every since the Sedona trip the paparazzi had again taken to following Julian and photographing his every move. It didn't bring work and he got no revenue from it. There were times when he thought he should do a reality show where he would get paid for being filmed, but it couldn't last past one day. Blue. Depressed. Story told. Grey Mars carefully followed the online coverage, sighing even as he blocked it from Julian's view.

"What is it?" Julian asked.

"Space alien hook up to take the Aurora Borealis flight home."

"I have no idea what that means," Julian said, worrying not over the innocuous press—it was nothing compared with the anxiety he was feeling over meeting with his stern, *Snömannen*, his wild-man father again after all these years of near silence.

"Why the lemons?" Mars asked about the small crate Julian brought with him. He made no mention of the larger crate of apples they lugged along, too.

"He asked for lemons from my California tree. He assumes I have one. Listen, Grey, my father is not going to be anything like you imagine. He's grisly."

"What do you imagine I imagine? My father was a pretty bleak guy, Juli."

"Old, strong, mean, remember the mean, and don't turn you back on him, and don't enter any type of contest with him. He cannot stand to lose," Julian cautioned.

"Like one of your trolls?"

"Hush Grey! Do not speak of things you can't know," Julian said looking around for any omen of evil. There were certain things to be believed in.

By now they were on the ground, in the sparse land of the Svalbard archipelago that island near Norway, above the arctic circle, an expectedly barren place. Winter had pulled back for a few weeks, taking much of its snow, but it was cold. Longyearbyen, made cheerful by the bright colors every structure and house was painted, but still an unornamented village, sat in the flat pan of the surrounding mountain ranges. The landscape was barren, and all rough edges and laden with a gloomy, intricate past that Julian hoped Mars already knew so he would not have to explain anything about this forsaken mining town newly popular with scientists and tourists. His father's connection to the mines was probably something terrible, and profitable.

The trip from the airport to the hotel was short, probably less than a mile, but they were bundled into a van and driven to the door probably because the laws regarding polar bears had become quite strict. No one wanted another tourist eaten alive. No one wanted to kill a bear. The driver carried a high-powered, large game rifle for that purpose. No one, Julian noted, carried anything like a machine gun. They pulled into the hotel parking lot.

"This it? Already?" Grey Mars asked, chuckling. "Looks like a space ship."

"I haven't been here since I was a boy," Julian said clutching the crate of lemons.

"Seems like you don't want to get out of the van, either. You afraid of something?" Mars asked, but quietly, like he was already formulating an escape plan. Julian stepped out, taking his box of lemons with him.

"Funny how you never notice trees until you visit a place that doesn't have any. This place looks nuclear bomb-blasted it is so God damn bare."

"Most of the archipelago is iceberg, I think. With only a very few animals, but the polar bears can come from anywhere this time of year so be careful," Julian said, trying to sound off hand. Before the trip, he couldn't bring himself to review the latest news of Longyearbyen, which was never home to him. This strange meeting place only made him more tense and suspicious of his father's motives.

Mars's clicked pictures without his usual narration (holy shit! Will you look at that! There's a great shot!), pretending to be engrossed in the meager landscape, the neat rows of identically structured box houses, set apart from one another by only their vibrant colors, nodding frequently while Julian tried to keep the lid on his quietly-frantic state.

Julian wrung his blue hands before stuffing them back in his gloves. The ground was bare. The only snow left was sitting on

42

the caps and in the folds of the surrounding mountains. They packed light, wearing most of their clothes already. A Californian for so many years now, Julian had lost his insulation against the arctic. He was grateful that it was still cold enough to be wrapped in a hooded jacket, with a scarf wrapped around his face. For this trip, he'd brought more pairs of sunglasses than books. The clean air was like an astringent. It raked at his lungs, made the whites of his eyes burn. The feeling of homesickness for the filthy air of Los Angeles made him quiver with longing for the stale heat and freeways clogged with so many stupid, erratic drivers he usually wanted them all imprisoned, or deported back to the Midwest. And yet, there was something in the cold, dry air that dragged his feet harder onto the earth. He lifted each foot, checked the bottom of his boots for magnets, and then looked around to see who was watching.

"Look, Juli, it's midnight and the sun is still out. The midnight sun," Mars cried, delighted. "Mountain, after bare mountain. Volcanoes? This place looks like the desert. Remember Phoenix? What was this place before, a military base?"

"Worse, a coal mining town. It might still be. I don't know any more."

The Svelbard Archipelago had a complicated history involving Germans, Russians, whaling, mining, a world war, with no doubt buckets of blood sloshed all around. Americans had such a different perspective on history, specifically World War II, and the aftermath, than he had been taught, there really was no safe comment to be made. Julian pulled his lips together, adjusted his scarf carefully shielding his face.

"So I'm guessing that is not a ski lift?" Mars gestured toward the series of skeletal towers that followed the contour of the mountain nearest them. Julian shook his head woodenly.

"Come on Juli, how bad can your father be?" Mars whispered, turning his back to the entourage of men that arrived on behalf of Julian's father to escort them to the hotel as soon as they got off the plane. To a man, they carried the high-power rifles.

"My mother told me once that when she was thirteen my father did something very bad to her and I became the result, and so they had to be married. It was the way there. Then."

Of course they could both imagine what that would have been. Mars shifted his weight over his feet. He took a knitted hat from his jacket pocket, and pulled it over his head.

"So what's the language here?" He asked, a hand on Julian's shoulder.

"Some version of Norwegian. It isn't a very uniform language," Julian answered, appreciating the change of subject. "Probably German, and Russian. Swedish, and English, no doubt Danish."

"What's the population?"

"A couple thousand, I believe."

The two porters from inside the hotel began talking among themselves quietly, but now in Swedish. They were getting the luggage, the crates of fruit. Julian spoke to them as minimally as possible, embarrassed by his clumsy use of his native language, his scant understanding of their deeper conversations, which he thought involved money, a particular woman, and gambling.

"Why do they all keep saying, 'tackle a midget'? Isn't that just *wrong*?" Mars asked.

"*Tack själv!* I believe it's means thank you," Julian said quietly.

Grey let the hungry hyena laugh out, and pointed his camera around shooting everything. It was probably the first time it had failed to make Julian laugh, too. "Norwegian is not the same as Swedish then? Shouldn't it be?"

"It's all fruit from the same tree, I suppose. But no, my language is not Swedish, but we can usually understand each other. After getting past the accents, the colloquialisms, the burning competitiveness to over rule, perhaps even murder, one another. The Swedes call a banana, *banana*. In Norway it's called a *yellow bend*. Have to keep some things toward national pride and all." His voice shook; no matter how he bent his thoughts to it, he could not steady it. "Everybody wants to keep his culture pure. It's not always a sweet, white smile on a beautiful blonde," He said feebly, all the sharp sarcasm gone. He didn't want to get into any discussion about the national resistance to any type of immigration, let alone integration. Once they were inside, their bags were set on the floor, the crates of fruit on the large coffee table in the lobby.

Julian exchanged a politely friendly goodbye, tipped them, and watched them leave with relief.

The lobby doors opened again, and another small group of big, rough old men entered. Each looked carved from an ancient tree. Julian sensed his father was one among them, but he couldn't be absolutely certain which man it was until he heard him speak. Julian recognized his father by his voice, prepared his brain to flip the switch into thinking in his first language, the only way he could avoid the torturous in-his-head translating. His father was still as large as he remembered. Julian was certain that under his bulky clothes they had identical builds, shoulders straight across, his spine, perpendicular, as if there were a coat hanger still inside the jacket. Julian was certain if he pressed his fist into his father's gut he would hit solid muscle. From the neck up, was the old man. His face was craggy, like a dried prune with harsh blue headlights in place of his eyes. The strong jaw-- Julian's jaw line, too-- was outlined with scraggly grey whiskers. Julian didn't have any idea how old he was, but thought he remembered being told he was over sixty at the time of his birth.

"*Du er min sønn*," his father said to him. Feeling discovered, Julian nodded.

They did not hug, but his father knocked his hood down. That fist came too near his eye; Julian flinched.

"Why are you blue?" Someone asked, surprised, and in perfect English.

"Mercury poisoning," Mars said quickly, his new standard answer for Julian. This explanation seemed to satisfy one member of the press in Oslo, so Mars had stuck with it.

Mars got between them first and introduced himself in the only language he knew, and for some reason, Julian's father, Lars Lunden responded back in English, and maintained the entire conversation making very few errors.

Later, in the hotel's small restaurant while they were waiting for their plates of reindeer, scalloped potatoes, and other dishes Julian hadn't eaten in years, his father took one of the lemons wiped it on his shirt and bit into it, smacking his lips with delight. The man ate the whole thing, skin and all and then dared anyone watching to do the same. When no one took him up on this, he took the apples and snapped them in half, handing them out to everyone, like prizes. They all ate the apple halves, as they had cleaned their dinner plates with attention to detail. Afraid of what his father might want, Julian struggled through the meal. Beer, and ice-cold vodka flowed all night.

Eventually Julian and Grey managed to extricate themselves from the table, but not without Julian's father giving him ten minutes of terse instructions in Norwegian. They hurried away.

"We are to meet him here at five am," Julian reported to Mars.

"It's already five am. Does he mean tomorrow morning?"

Julian slapped a hand to his head, turned around and went to speak to his father.

"We'll meet him at noon, in the lobby," Julian said to Grey, laughing a little. "He wants to show us around. I wish he would just tell me what he wants."

Grey Mars said, "If eating that raw lemon was some warriors move to make his opponents feel weak, it fucking worked. I also have an apple in my pocket to see if I can snap it in half with my bare hands in the room. How you holding up?"

"He is exactly as I remembered," Julian said, feeling unaccountably saddened by this.

After that they went to their separate rooms. Julian heard Mars start snoring almost immediately so he wondered if his friend even bothered to undress, let alone try to snap that apple in half. Julian could not sleep, took a sleeping pill, which didn't work, and then tried some cough syrup with codeine, but that didn't work. His mind whirled, but would not shut off so by the time they met his father and the four other men who accompanied him, his brain was wobbling between drunkenness, the drugs, stress and every type of physical exhaustion that jet lag brings on.

Mars came crashing out of his room almost shouting, "I have a headache the size of the full moon! I brushed my teeth six times and my mouth still feels rancid. So tell me, what's this place like."

"Except for the polar bears, probably the safest place on earth," Julian said. He was still trying to understand why he had come. Self-supporting since his university days, his father had no

46

real claim on him anymore, he was a grown man, why did he agree to this trip.

They met in the lobby and walked to one of the larger clapboard houses. This one was painted the color of a mint, nothing like the brighter houses.

"It's the law to carry a rifle outside the settlement in case of a polar bear attack. If you see one, shoot right away. You can't outrun them."

Julian was handed a rifle, but not Mars, something that clearly insulted him, something obvious only to Julian. Mars was also raised on deer hunting, but everyone assumed he knew nothing of this kind of more earthbound world. Julian handed him his rifle.

"Let the fucker eat me and shit me out in the ocean. The circle of life," Julian said wearily.

"Don't be morbid, Juli," Mars said running his hand down the barrel, the stock, checking the mechanisms, before he released and checked the clip before snapping it back in and shouldering the gleaming rifle.

Instead of going to the mines, as Julian had thought, they were going to climb through an ice cave, geographical features Julian had occasionally explored during his cold, lonely childhood. No one bothered to explain why. Two of the men went in first, no doubt checking for bears, foxes, or other people before they all ascended into the frozen underworld.

This is where they separated. Julian's father pulled him into a niche, cold, and lined with icicles.

"Drink this!" He demanded shoving a Thermos at Julian. "Drink it all."

Julian chugged down what tasted like strong coffee, laced with some kind of alcohol with the high octane of gasoline. The aftertaste was boiled seaweed and something disgustingly earthy, like ground patchouli. As soon as it hit his empty belly, it burned through his veins, his heart reacted immediately. Julian turned to his father, wanted to ask him, what is this, but his tongue would not leave his mouth. Every part of him seemed to shrug.

"Will your skin change again? Are you used to being blue?" his father asked.

"I'm used to it until I look at my own hands," Julian answered evenly.

"Then wear gloves," his father said.

"Yes," Julian breathed. "That's exactly what it is like. A life of wearing gloves."

His father said: *"Julian, komme hjem sønn."*

The torches turned off, everything went black. "Come home son," his father repeated, and kept talking, his words became incomprehensible burrowing deep into his primitive brain. Someone patted his back, further tamping the cold into his bones. His mother, he thought, a daisy on the frozen tundra, blowing silently in the cold, dry wind of his harsh father. After that he began walking through his dream. Above them a waterfall poured. Mr. Charlie Walbridge stood on the bank, looking nonplussed at the newly pinned kayak, bright red, against the stone, flipped on its side. They all knew if was full of water, that was a given. You cannot imagine the heat of a jungle, the wetness, the difficulty moving through it, the constant chirping. Julian crossed his arms across his chest, cupped an elbow in each palm.

Mr. Walbridge stood on the bank of the river, rubbing his hands together, "we'll free it. It'll have a crease, but that's not the point. Freedom is the point."

The gospel spoken, everyone nodded seriously. Julian thought Mr. Walbridge made a good god.

"The Z-drag," he finally announced. They all waited for more. "A Z-Drag is a three-to-one mechanical advantage hauling system that can be set up with a few lightweight tools you all brought. We'll throw on a brake prusik. Let's get started, everyone back in your helmets, PFDs, no barefeet, and let's all take this seriously," he advised, arms crossed over his chest, like he had the slim book memorized, and, unlike Julian he was not clowning the instructions to break the tension. The men obeyed to every letter, the boat was extracted more efficiently than Julian expected. Everyone cheered.

Julian grew so hot standing there watching the tropics sweat through its leaves, his armpits felt on fire. He needed a cooling swim. Rolling to his hip first, he stood, and kept climbing out until he reached the earth warming in midnight sun. The seawater lay obediently in the bay, grey and flat and hardly riffled by wind. He peeled his coat off, and then his shirt, letting them fall to the ground soundlessly like clouds bumping into the mountains. The white gleam broke the surface of the gray water, and began to grow out of it, a head, massive. What felt like thousands of broken needles were traveling through his bloodstream. Julian walked toward the cold water.

"Jesus! Fuck! Juli! Run!" Mars cried.

Shots cracked the sky, something hot hit his back. He wiped at the spot where he felt the most pain, and was sickened by red blood on his blue skin. Lizardman, the word crawled through his brain.

At the hospital, after the surgery, Grey Mars stood alone by his bedside.

"Do you think my father shot me on purpose?" Julian asked.

"If he was aiming for that bear he needed a scope, a compass, and someone to tap on his shoulder and point the way."

"Did he get arrested?"

"I told the police I didn't see how you got shot, I was too busy aiming at the bear. I don't know what happened after we left. Do you remember the helicopter?"

Miraculously, the bullet missed everything he needed to live, it was a through and through. *Gjennom og gjennom.*

Mars leaned in as closely as he could. "Do you think he got you there to try and kill you? Because you are blue?"

"Yes. And too bad he missed my heart."

"For fuck sakes, Juli, what the hell were you doing out there? I had to kill a bear."

"Grey, I was sleepwalking. I had jet lag. When I couldn't sleep I took those pills, and then I drank this cough syrup. In that cave, my father ordered me to drink something. I don't know what happened after that," he said, hating the sound of excuses. He shouldn't have dragged Mars along. That was the truth. They should not have come.

Mars looked exhausted, but he had obviously cleaned up and combed his hair while he was waiting for Julian to awaken. The cup of coffee he held still steamed, freshly poured. This scent of the fresh brew, strong Norwegian coffee made Julian long to get home, into his couch cave and suffer in silence.

"I'm just worried about the Karma," Grey said seriously. His eyes were down but they flickered nervously around the room as if he were next. "That bear came out of the water like someone was calling it," Mars whispered.

Julian sighed. "They spend most of their lives in the water, hunting seals and fish. And I do remember saying I wouldn't mind getting eaten by one. Maybe he was summoning up my wish."

"Juli, I would trade places with you in a minute, just to relieve both of our suffering. I really think I could not only live with being blue, but I'd enjoy being different."

Julian nodded. "I should not have brought you. I should never have come back here."

"Do I need to put you on a suicide watch?" Mars whispered. "I have to leave for England in just a few hours."

"No. Just let me sleep. I'll be fine. I will start seeing a psychiatrist now. You can rest easy. I won't let you down, Grey."

"With your permission, I'm going to make sure that demented old man can't get near you," Mars said.

"He won't come here. I'll never see him again," Julian said, weary.

"I'm going to make sure of it. I'll call you when I land," Mars patted the pillow next to Julian's head.

"It's a shame you couldn't see the real Norway, it's so beautiful."

"Some day we will. That fucker can't live forever."

After that Julian pretended to slip into a coma. Grey Mars flew off to England to see to his work. Later, when Grey Mars retold this tale all the disgraceful parts—a man shooting his suicidal blue son—would be ingeniously elided, the actual events twisted so subtly it would make whoever heard it laugh. That was Grey Mars's gift. Julian wished he would be able to hear it retold, but of course he never would.

A nurse came in to make adjustments on the I.V. tubes, take his vital signs, clean his wound, sponge him off. She was older, the grey was beginning to filter into her pale hair. Rini was gentle. It was easy to pretend she wasn't there. Julian was reading a book Mars had left him, an old-fashioned story, *Evalina*, which made Julian wonder what Mars was really up to these days.

"My name is Rini," she said with an accent Julian could not be certain of. "You know, I recognized you right away. You are a wonderful actor."

"Thank you." He had to admit to himself, he liked that she didn't say *were an actor* in the past tense.

"Your nice friend, that one with the name of the planet, told me you were depressed over this change in skin color. And you are very healthy, other than this gunshot hole in your side, which is healing rapidly because of your sturdy health. Did you know that?"

"I don't know what I know anymore," Julian said, and this made him think of Talia, who he would call back if he weren't this pitiful blue. He snuck a peak at his hand, why did he have to be such an undeniable shade of blue?

"You know I won't tell you about the young man losing his leg to cancer or the children suffering their tumors of the brain and liver. Julian, all you need is love. We are not meant to be alone. Why don't you make another movie?" She chided him gently massaging his arm.

"I tried a play. People won't want to see me in blue skin," Julian confessed.

"Oh, one play? I read about that. Ill conceived, but that is the director's fault, not the actors. Make another movie! After a few minutes, no one will notice. You disappear into your characters," she said this so sincerely Julian put his hand on hers to make sure she was really there. People would not overlook his blue. Skin color mattered.

"You were blue in that Aqua Man the entire time. There is so much more story there. And now the curiosity factor would bring in new fans."

"Are you a Hollywood agent disguised as a nurse?" Julian asked. This sent Rini into fits of laughter that made her face flush red.

"Do you want more pain medication?" She asked.

"No. I'm not in pain. Please, I need to clear my head," Julian said.

In two days all the drugs had left his system-- he supposed the IV of clear fluids that ran into his arm helped with that—the world came into sharp focus again. There were a couple of moments when he felt a tickle of excitement in his belly, over what he could not name. Thoughts of his parents were again easily vanquished, and he didn't so much as forgive his father, but deliberately wipe him out of his conscious memory. Sometimes this took extreme perseverance and distraction.

The small hospital room had three pieces of furniture including the bed. Even the walls were shiny it was that immaculate and without a single blush of colorful to distract the ill. There was no television. Clearly, they did not expect to distract patients from healing, in any way.

"Do you have anything to read?" Julian held up the beat up copy of *Evalina*, testament to how desperate he was. *Save me from Evalina and her comedic, but important life altering faux pas. Evalina taking in the refreshing air and soul enriching beauty of a near Eden of a garden when she is attacked by a drunken sailor, and rescued by prostitutes. Whatever would be the greater humiliation?* Only his pity for writers kept him from throwing the book down.

"Ah, I have some wonderful books. I'll bring them right back," the nurse said. She returned within an hour with a stack of paperbacks.

"I think you might find these inspiring, in their own way," she said, carefully placing them on the tiny square of bedside table. Julian picked up Homer's, *The Odyssey,* a book he always claimed to have read, but never had.

After that, they talked in short bursts, when she had a few spare minutes throughout the day. For dessert after lunch she brought him some puzzling foods, like fig pudding, which he pretended to like, half fearing she would bring him seconds. Julian autographed a copy of *Evalina* she dug up somewhere even though he tried to explain the copy he had was not his pick, but the handsome Mr. Planet she kept referring to. She also asked him to autograph a piece of fabric for her using a special pen.

"This is the best cotton I could find. I'm going to embroider over your signature and turn this into the edge of my new favorite pillowcase," her cheeks blushed small starfish of pink when she said this, but otherwise she seemed unabashed. While she watched with a nurse's skilled eye, he signed it with great care trying to anticipate the looping of colorful thread over his marks.

"What you need is love, Julian," Rini said this to him often enough so that he knew she meant it as an unwritten prescription he must somehow fill. He promised her he would work on it, yet he knew he couldn't. There was never a time he'd felt in love with anyone. The vase of brilliant orange flowers she brought were such a relief from the immaculate white, Julian could hardly take his eyes off of them.

"Has anyone telephoned your mother?"

"She disappeared many years ago when I left for boarding school," Julian said, unable to elaborate even in his own mind the uneven attempts of his mother to love him. "My father is a cruel man. She wouldn't want to be found. Not while he is alive anyway." This was the most he had ever told anyone about her.

"God protect her," Rini said.

"What can you tell me about your life?"

"I have a very small, green house," she explained. "My son and husband built it with old wooden windows from the salvage. It's glorious."

Julian told her that it had to be.

"I also brought you a nice dish of *muschi poiana*."

Julian wasn't certain what that was, but the delicious scent of it, coupled with the intent of the gesture: genuine mothering, brought tears to his eyes.

"Sorry," he sniveled, wiping his nose on the crisp white sheet.

"You are going to be emotional," she brought a box of tissue out of nowhere. "Two big traumas, snip, snap. It's not a good time for you to be alone. Maybe you can take some therapy when you get home?"

He promised her he would consider it, but he knew he wouldn't do it. Therapy terrified Julian. There was too much buried under all those trembling, brittle layers, he didn't want to know what all. The next time she came in Julian asked her if she wanted to do a scene with him from one of her favorite movies.

"Ah! Yes, and maybe I can make a voice recording to listen to when I lay my head on my special pillowcase?"

Afterward, they applauded each other. "You're pretty good!" Julian said, making the pink starfish rise to her cheeks again. Next, they did a few short scenes from Shakespeare. Rini adored the scenes in Romeo and Juliet where the nurse was on stage. Of course she played the nurse. A part, Julian told her, she was born to play, just to see the starfish come out. Julian played whatever other parts were needed.

Nurse: Out upon you, what a man are you?
Romeo: One, gentlewoman, that God hath made, himself to mar.
Nurse: By my troth, it is well said: "for himself to mar," quoth 'a!

The simplicity of their mutual enjoyment and quiet homage to the art of these important plays made him cry outright. "There, there," Rini reassured him by massaging his calves. And in the quiet hush of night, Rini told Julian about nursing during the Chechen wars. Acting as a physician in a gutted, practically abandoned hospital. "So many landmines, Juli, the limbs have to be sawed off, stitched closed. Just the one doctor. I learned so much. Here, I am permitted to hand an IV bag." She cried silently into her open hand. "I am so glad for it, to just be able to *heal* my patients. Sometimes when a bad case seems like a lost cause and they live, I feel I gave birth to them. Silly, I know." There were no more details after that. They ran scenes together and feasted on her unusual cooking.

Of course Grey Mars called a couple of times a day, always beginning with:

"Juli, I was such a shit head worrying about shooting a bear when my best friend was shot by his own father!" It didn't seem like he could say anything else when he heard Julian's voice when he desperately wanted to know why Mars was reading the almost-deadly sentimental novel, *Evelina*, but he could not ask.

"Promise we'll never speak of it again," Julian said every time.

"Promise," Mars always replied, but of course he spoke of it every time he called, and this often brought more tears to Julian's eyes. He rubbed those away on the white sheet, too, a sturdy fabric much more soothing than the paper tissue.

At some point during his brief stay a doctor in an immaculate lab coat, appeared holding an electronic tablet. One year Julian had received several tablets as gifts, but he never understood how they got so popular. Before any other conversation took place he asked Julian if he might make a photograph of him.

"No, you may not," Julian snapped, mainly because he hated the expression, *make a photograph.*

The doctor's response was to tap onto the screen of his tablet while he informed Julian that his rate of healing was remarkable. Obviously, because he had such superior health parameters, he should live to be quite old, he was told. *Record breaking old*, he said this like a god bestowing a gift. The doctor wanted to include Julian in a longitudinal study on aging, how did Julian feel about that?

Julian despaired: what did he want with a longer life?

## Chapter Six

Alone with his thoughts, Julian reasoned that in his lifetime his father had done worse things than shoot him when he was on the verge of suicide anyway. Maybe he felt he was saving him from a cursed afterlife. In fact, the whole incident had sobered him from the idea of killing himself so maybe he had done him a favor. The worst moments were picturing his father's lined face, and burning eyes asking him when he was going to get rid of that lizard skin. Julian would never speak to his father again, he decided. Never.

During the long flight home he devoured the books Rini had given him as parting gifts. Julian paused often in his reading to search the covers of the books, wondering if she had carefully selected each specifically as hints. The stories seemed to stir some ideas in him, ideas for screenplays he might write, and produce. Whatever became of this new seed of excitement, he realized he wanted to live. In return for the books, as they said goodbye, he promised to write, to stop drinking, to refuse the pain medication. Since he had nothing else, he had given her his Skype number, so they could still run scenes, and his email address, begging her to keep in touch. And then in the moment, he had given her the golden cross his father had placed in his hand as they were packing him into the air ambulance, saying it was something his mother had left behind. Just then it seemed the only thing he had to give her that seemed right. Each of the four points glinted from her neck as she fingered it, like it had finally been returned to its rightful owner, and maybe it had.

"And just one more thing," she said. "I don't think you should wear that hood on your jacket up any more, Julian. Look at this. And I only show you so you will see. Someone left this in the nurses lounge."

She had handed him a worn, well-thumbed magazine, a rag turned to a page in which a shot of Julian in his hoody, was next to a film still, a blue evil villain from an older movie. Both in their hoodies, blue faces tucked back, wide eyes radiating shame, or fear, or maybe just your basic self-consciousness, Julian couldn't tell anymore.

A black man in blue face, Julian mused. *Electro*, Julian made a mental note to get the DVD as soon as he got back.

"I think he looks better," Julian quipped.

"He is supposed to look evil. You are not evil," Rini said seriously.

On his way home, Julian left the hood down, and if only that made everything good and fine as it should have been, but it was disaster.

From the safety of his living room he could, without panic attack, relive the scene in the Oslo airport. Julian jogged his way through to show his good health and to outrun the newly aroused Paparazzi, but they seemed to increase in numbers until a old man stood up and asked him, in Norwegian, "do you want them to take your picture?" Uncertain of where he should go, Julian shook his head. The man placed himself in front of Julian and then so did another dozen of people and then another dozen joined in. Many voices began to shame the Paparazzi until the security came and as a human fence. This collection of people escorted Julian to his departure gate. Oh people, my people, Julian thought once he was safely tucked into his first class window seat, breathing heavily. Mars had paid for that seat and Julian had paid for the one next to it so he didn't have to make anyone uncomfortable if they were seated next to him. He set his books on it, took off his shoes and read his way home.

At the airport his gardener picked him up in his enormous white pick up truck. The bed was, as usual, filled with ladders, rakes, hoes, hoses, a mower and an assortment of weed-whackers. The short trailer attached to the truck was full of green cuttings, palm tree fronds, juniper branches, and mounds of cut grass wrapped in white tarps. When Julian had called to ask him for the lift home the gardener didn't hesitate to tell him he would be there on time. At the airport curb he got out to open the door for him.

"*Senor Azul como fue?*" He asked genially.

"Well, Alejandro, my father shot me-- *Mi papa me disparo.*"

The gardener laughed like he understood how those things went.

For a few days after that Julian seemed to relax into his new blue life. Mars, now in Scotland, called regularly, but clearly, he was homesick.

"Juli, I'm becoming a wrung out version of myself. I'm a rag, as colorless as the sky here. I'm fucking hate rain for good now. My feet have mold on them. I can't wait to get back under the golden California sun, and breathe deeply of the smog."

After reading the book Mars had left behind, Julian had just read hints in the trades, and he was worried. "Grey, you aren't seriously thinking of making *Evalina* into a movie?"

"You don't love the idea?"

"I hate the idea," Julian laughed. "I'm certain I can guess whose idea this is, too."

Mars made a rattling noise, like he was trying to clear his throat of half chewed apples. Then the hungry hyena laugh slammed into Julian's ear, making him smile. The real Grey was out. "You caught me it's her idea." *Her* was Grey's new name for his wife, but he stammered on the word, so it came out with the vowel smeared, a subtle shift that told Julian his friend was at that emotional crossroad where he would either free float to space on over-inflated happiness, or crash to the center of the earth, despairing. Julian knew it well, this caused him to slap at his own chest trying to free it of the sting. As usual, he did not know what to say.

"You seriously don't like the idea?"

"Terrible idea." Julian said flatly. "Unless you want to hoist yourself by your own petard."

"I've never understood that expression."

"Petard is French for bomb. It means blow yourself up with your own stupidity."

"I do that every twenty minutes. And listen, Juli, why don't you come out of the blue pity zone and write me a fucking script I can use."

"I might just try my hand at it."

"Write yourself into a part," Grey said. "The true fans are waiting. And you're right. It's a terrible idea. I couldn't get past page ten. That's why I left it for you. I had to use Cliff Notes to answer all of her questions." Mars let the hungry hyena out, making Julian laugh, too.

They talked on quivery long distance for twenty more minutes, mainly on safe, polite matters of health weather and the finer people looking out for each of them in their strange lands.

"I'll be back in two more weeks. What say we go over your pages then?"

"My pages? Okay, I'll write. I'll finish," Julian promised. "Sci fi."

"Email me the premise and if you got some pages, send those too…"

Reluctant to let go, they talked for another ten minutes with Grey Mars lamenting the weather, the accents, the backass driving, and other odds and ends that made him laugh, although half-heartedly, a fed hyena, or sleepy. Julian didn't know how to describe it. This was as negative as he had ever heard his friend.

Three weeks later Julian still replayed this conversation in his head as he ran through Laurel Canyon. The pages for his screenplay were shaping up. Of course Mars wanted to see them as they were finished, but Julian wanted to give him the complete first draft when he got home. Grey Mars was due to land that day, Julian was trying to get it all down.

At Happy Lane he paused and looked up. A black crow resting on the sign flapped his wings at Julian. A car whooshed by, someone shouted, "freak!" as they threw a cup of coffee out the window. The dark liquid mess landed at his heels and splashed up his bare legs. While Julian was still turned around assessing the reach of the coffee stains, Alejandro pulled up in his gardener's rig, only this time the double cab was filled with men.

"Senor Azul, you okay?"

Julian nodded.

"Don't worry my boys here got the plate number."

"Don't call the police, it'll bring more cameras," Julian said.

"No, no police," Alejandro said waving his hand. The men inside nodded seriously. Julian should've told them not to bother, but he thought he could use some revenge carried out on his behalf.

"I got cold beer when you come by today," Julian said.

"You want a lift back?"

Julian shook his head, gave the door a pat and they all separated. After considering it for a few minutes, he decided to finish his short walk by looping back and jogging on the edge of the steep, narrow road against traffic so no one could approach him blindly from behind. He was glad to get home, where his heart beat normally. All in all, he felt good.

The hose near his pool was neatly coiled into a contraption that kept it neatly hidden away, but didn't make it easy to get out or put back. While he hosed the coffee off the back of his legs, the sudden squawking of jays brought his attention up. Hawks circled overhead, a smaller bird flew into his enormous picture window, something that happened frequently, but for some reason, it filled Julian with a sense of dread. All that afternoon he sat on the observation deck on the roof of his house in which he could see that distinctive arrangement of the buildings, at this distance a glimmer darker than the smog that shrouded downtown Los Angeles, facing LAX. In one of the trees a squirrel chirped relentlessly, Julian wished he'd find his mate and leave the birds to their more pleasant bickering. Suddenly, his neck felt like solid wood, he could not turn his head, Julian kept the phone in his lap, waiting.

Early evening began arriving with its distinctive streak of orange on the horizon. Overhead a bright light appeared in the sky, Julian held his breath to see if it would move: plane or satellite. The light of a real star had not been able to cut its way through the city this early in forty years. Julian could only clutch the phone in his lap, still waiting. Finally, it was Grey Mars's assistant who told Julian that Mars was in critical condition, not expected to live. Springing out of the chair, he ran to his bedroom to dress while he was told the name of the hospital. Silently he mapped the route in his head. Just as he got his shirt on the doorbell began clanging over and over and over. One click on the computer and he could clearly see, via the security cameras that surrounded his property, that it was the police at his front gate, but he did not want to let them in; did not want to hear anything from them about Grey Mars. After ten minutes, a woman identifying herself as a dispatcher called him to ask him if he would let the police in his front gate. Stalling, Julian asked her for proof and a series of questions, his senses heightened for a quick get away. The black and white patrol car was blocking his garage doors, so he couldn't ease past them. If they were there to tell him that Mars was dead, he had no choice but to hear it from them.

Eventually he went down, and opened the gate, but kept them inside his mid-century modern stone courtyard waving for them to sit in the chairs that were arranged around a palm, low fountain, and other modern sculptures the architect thought were essential for framing the enormous front doors. One of them said, "Ah the blue man," but they kept their distance, obviously slightly suspicious of his color, too, like he was deliberately trying to present himself as some sort of blue dissident.

They asked if he knew Grey and when he said yes. They told his about Grey's accident.

"Critical," Julian repeated.

"He's married, but he's listed you as next of kin, as his emergency contact."

"I'm trying to go to the hospital now," Julian said.

"Are you his relative?"

Briefly, and with an actor's candor he told them of his business relationship with Mars. There were no words to explain how much a brother Grey Mars was to him.

"We are close friends, too," Julian said feebly.

They reacted casually as if this was they expected to hear. There was always the hint that Julian was gay, but he never cared, still didn't. In the past it had made Mars laugh, too. Just the idea of the two of them trying to 'get it on' as Mars had chuckled. "If only people knew how much time and money I spend chasing pussy. It has to be easier being gay." Maybe people believed that if they could frame Julian as gay they would know something deep about him, but that wasn't true. The yard lights came on, highlighting the small vignettes in his rather exotic courtyard, an indication that time was definitely passing. He had to get to Mars, he thought, his throat clenching. By that time the keys in his hand felt foreign, and he almost pocketed them, but instead started shaking them impatiently.

"How can I help you?" He asked.

"We found a gun in the car. It was registered to you," one of the men in a suit told him. Julian waited for him to finish, but when he didn't said, "And?" The silence left them all staring at each other, like they were waiting to see who's would come up with the next case-cracking question. Julian continued to give them his stone face. Dark crept around their feet, everyone moved into a tighter circle where the light illuminated the plants. Soon, more lights would blink on automatically. Would he need an attorney to get them off his property?

"Why did Mr. Mars have it?" The one woman among them finally asked, her face tipped like it was one of those clever cocktail hour questions.

"Was he shot with it?" Julian began to worry that Grey Mars being slowly roasted on a spit somewhere, after suffering from a gunshot wound, some mad karma from killing the polar bear. Of its own free will his hand slipped to his forehead, testing for heat; he worried he might be hallucinating. The one thing Julian knew for certain was that Grey Mars could never harm anyone. That killing of the bear still weighed so heavily on Mars, the dreams tortured him so well that during their last conversation he had admitted to donating thousands of dollars to the research station in Svalbard.

"The clip is missing," she said again like she was finally putting the punch line to the joke, and the wrong punch line at that.

"I still don't understand why you are here," Julian said.

"Why did he have it?" Someone asked.

Julian decided to act like he had just cracked under the pressure of their carefully managed interrogation.

"Grey Mars is my best friend. My brother, really. Shortly after I became blue, he realized I was suicidal. One day when I was especially depressed he took the gun out of the house."

"Why would you be thinking about suicide?"

Julian held up his hands. "I had just turned blue. You were reluctant to shake hands with me. It's depressing let me tell you. Now, you tell me why are you here?"

No one seemed to want to answer that. By now Julian was weary of the shuffling, the heavily spaced questions. The sense of doom enveloped him.

"Is he dead?" Julian asked.

One of them fiddled with his phone, read the screen, looked up said, "No. Still in surgery."

"Please go. I have to see to my friend," he said quietly. They told him where he could pick up gun.

"Melt it," Julian said.

Grey was still in surgery when Julian arrived, no one would venture an opinion about how well his friend might come through, and this left him pacing in a small circle around the small metal chair he'd pulled next to the huge double doors that led to the operating rooms. In contrast to his recent stay in a hospital, that was spare, utilitarian, radiating with its own white cleanliness, this hospital was a monument to the gods that worked inside. The waiting room chairs were colorfully upholstered, the signs, gold lettered, there were in-house coffee bars, and a world-class art collection hanging down its long, pale, tastefully painted, pastel corridors, all donations from wealthy patients-- he couldn't care less. He finally sat in the chair, hiding his blue hands inside the pockets of his jacket, trying to hear Grey Mars letting his hyena laugh out. The hospital workers who passed him usually pretended they didn't see him. Now and again someone would nod, or say, "Blue Man." They didn't intrude. For that he was immeasurably grateful. Time inched along with no word, Julian tried to remember the last conversation he'd had with Mars, and couldn't. Julian began to feel the weight of death, and this somehow tapped him down into sleep.

Awakening on the cold floor he slowly realized he was peering up the smock of a woman leaning on a mop. Her expression reminded Julian of Rini, someone he suddenly felt desperate to talk to. She would know what he should be doing for Mars.

"You fell out of your chair," she said, gripping the mop like she might go down next to him without it. "That guy over there is waiting for you to wake up." She rolled her eyes, before she turned to the pudgy guy nervously fingering the edge of his glasses. "He's awake now," she told him before sauntering off, that mop became a handle she used to steer the bucket on wheels with. Neither made any noise.

"Julian, hey, man you are truly blue! Hey, but nice to meet you. I'm Mr. Mars's new assistant. Dan. Dan the man."

Julian rubbed his forehead and sat up. "Do you know what happened to Grey?"

Now Dan the Man leaped over and squatted on the floor and began whispering.

"Some politician, I can't find out who YET, slammed into him, out of his mind drunk. Wasted. They're trying to keep it hush-hush. I'm worried about Mr. Mars. It's like they're trying to make it out as all his fault."

Conspiracy theories weren't normally something Julian leaned towards, but he could see how the police visit fit into all of it. They wanted Julian's story. Luckily, he didn't have one to give them.

"There was a clip to a gun, the police came by to ask me about it. Said Mrs. Mars had called in a complaint some weeks ago that Grey threatened her, and now she's disappeared," Dan-the-Man gushed.

"Where is Mrs. Mars?" Julian asked, trying to make sense of everything.

"Not a clue, she got pissed over something, or everything, packed up and vacated the house while Mr. Mars was in England. The problem is Julian, it's that Mr. Mars has some stuff happening, I mean important business that has to be attended to, but he keeps it all in his head. I should be in there covering for him."

Julian murmured that he understood, when actually he was thinking Grey gave him some steps to follow in case something like this were to happen, and he'd forgotten to keep his promise to quickly follow through.

"I'm going to make some calls," Julian told Dan-the-Man, before he slipped into an empty room and called the woman Mars trusted with everything. A woman, Julian would have sworn was a tough competitor of Grey's, but he was following instructions.

"Naomi, it's Julian Lunden," he choked, could not say Mars's name.

"I heard. I'm sick about Grey. Hang on, I'm gonna have to ball for a few minutes," she paused to sob. "Crap, but I have everything I need to cover his business so don't worry about it. I want to tell you two things, Julian: first, Mars thought of you as his only family, and he has been sick with worry that you would give up and leave him. I think you know what I mean. Any more guns, razor blades and the like at your place."

64

"He is my family," Julian repeated. "I'm not going to commit suicide."

"Good. I know you are a man of your word. Second thing. A couple of years ago, I had an aneurism, woke up one morning with a terrible headache and weeks later in the hospital, didn't know my own name or where I was. Mars could've destroyed me, but he stepped in and saved everything. Hold on, I'm gonna ball some more," she sobbed so hard Julian let go, too. "My kids were small. My husband is a good man, but he doesn't work, there's no getting around it. But it was the weirdest thing, Julian, the way he would come in and try to ask me about things. Like to try to get me to make a decision. I lost all my language. He would say, *Naomi, do you remember, say, Bill Doodle?* But my head was empty, like a kid's ball, all air. I knew I should know and that name would just travel through my mind all day long. I don't know how he took over so smoothly. He saved everything. I'll do that for him. And Julian you know me. I'll fucking kill for him after that."

"Yes, ok. I do know, Naomi. Let's have no more death of anything. Mars trusts you."

"And Julian, don't do anything selfish. Mars *will* wake up and he *will* expect to see that handsome blue face first thing."

"I'll be here waiting to be allowed in," Julian swore again.

Before he went home, Julian got to see Grey. The tubes and hoses, bandages and machines seemed to have him buried already, but he was alive. None of the doctors were very hopeful. Before he left- they only allowed him five minutes to stand at the foot of the bed in shock, he quickly took some photographs certain Grey would want to see how mangled he looked. The moment he was awake.

# Chapter Seven

Grey Mars remained in a coma for almost ten days before his wife showed up, wild eyed, her usually long and slick hair a frizzy mess, like she'd just driven miles in the convertible without a hat. Julian was shocked by how straw thin she was. Women did not realize how terrible it looked to see the outline of bones, where flesh was supposed to hide them. Her collarbone was so prominent it looked like her entire body was hung on a wire coat hanger. The skin looked wrapped around the bone, with no muscle, like a *dia de los muertos* skeleton.

"Where's the money Julian? And by the way, you look creepy all blue like that. Why don't you fix it?"

Naomi had already warned Julian that she would be on the warpath as soon as she realized that her allowance was now a well-defined, much smaller amount of money she could no longer expand with her newly restricted credit cards. The pre-nup was strict, and covered this kind of an event. The word 'abandoned' had tremendous power.

"What he sees in this woman," Naomi told Julian, who could only shrug in equal wonder. That was a part of Mars's life Julian put in his mental blind spot.

"Well she's in financial lock down, per Grey's explicit, written instructions," Naomi confided. "Also we had a sad conversation while he was in Scotland."

Naomi was one of those women who wore dark lipstick, but no make up otherwise. Rumor was that she was once an astonishing beauty, but let herself get a little fat so she would be taken seriously as a power broker, rather like the fat Buddha had done. Bucking against the stereotype she also wore expensive, untailored suits, with black and white oxfords.

"Nobody's grabbing that ass and keeping their arm," Grey used to say of Naomi.

In a grand mal temper tantrum the Mrs. Mars had locked them all out of Grey's room, the only thing, as wife, she had the power to do. On the way home, Julian called Naomi to see if there was anything she could do to restore Julian's visits. This was pure superstition, of course, but Julian felt certain Grey Mars would evaporate from the bed, leaving only the covers, tubes and bandages if he was not there to hang onto him.

"I'll work on it," Naomi said.

His body felt fit and strong, but the emotional weight that Grey Mars was injured beyond hope made him feel weak and flailing like an infant. Nothing he did could exhaust him enough to fall asleep. Julian went back to taking sleeping pills with a vodka chaser.

After doubling his run in miles and speed, Julian, afraid to miss a phone call, trotted back home to get some coffee while he kept the phone tucked in his armpit. His mid-century modern kitchen was designed for people who liked to give parties. The refrigerator, empty except for a carton of juice, eggs and a loaf of bread was enormous. If he removed the shelves, it was large enough for him to climb into, shut the door and silently suffocate in the cold. The thought always filled him with terror; tight closed spaces being one of the only things Julian feared. That and the wrath of Naomi. Also, Julian no longer wanted to die. He clumsily boiled water to fix a poached egg with toast. This he ate with three xanax, and a gigantic mug of vodka, a combination he was convinced helped him to think clearly. There was no need to dress, so he slept in his clothes. Julian took out his phone and paged through the call memory. Late into the night he talked to Rini, to Talia, to anyone who would pick up it seemed, even someone from some institute he never heard of. None of these conversations had calmed his anxious, alcohol-addled mind, not really, and they couldn't. He wanted to talk to Grey about Grey. He drank deeply directly from the bottle now.

After the vodka was gone, he ordered more groceries and booze via the Internet, using his usual list, it was five mouse clicks, and the delivery was paid and scheduled. On a pad by the phone, he had written some notes, for the most part they left him baffled. There were dollars signs, the word *study* and an adolescently crude drawing of an ass, crying tears. This he scribbled out, embarrassed. There was also a phone number written in his wobbling print at the bottom. He'd gone over and over the numbers, even coloring them in, so he guessed the call took a several minutes. Tapping the center of his forehead with his finger, he decided to call the institute back then because he thought-- no feared-- that he may have agreed to sell his sperm.

At the building he had been directed to, he had pulled into the back inside an unusual type of garage, where, as promised he was ushered in through a private door where no prying eyes could penetrate. Julian followed the short, burly man down the immaculate hallway.

"Did anyone get your picture coming in?" The man asked him, turning around.

"I haven't been bothered in awhile, so I'm hoping the world will just forget about me," Julian said.

"That would be a great blunder on the part of the science world, and the reason I asked you here. I intend to ensure that science does not stupidly let this opportunity pass."

Against his better judgment, Julian kept walking with him. It emerged that the doctor in Norway had contacted the institute in Culver City.

"I'm not a rat for study," Julian said.

"Of course not! You're a modern human, with an unsolved mystery, an incredible rate of healing, from your medical charts, you have never been sick. Not even a cold?"

Julian, feeling justifiably vulnerable made no response, not even a shrug, or a nod. His best friend was dying, without him. His heart was breaking, that was so much worse than a cold, but he said nothing. No one ever questioned his mental health.

"Wouldn't you like to help possibly cure disease?" The corridor they were walking down seemed to be flanked by two uninterrupted walls, yet Dr. Burrell paused and swung a door open, waving Julian in.

The doctor seemed to choose his words carefully, as if he were just trying out his excellent use of the English language. Julian was still reading Rini's sci-fi books, and thought it would be an excellent alien tongue for what he wanted to write. Finish the script, he told himself, so he had something to show Grey while he was healing. And then as he stepped inside the dark room, a light instantly came on and the thought flickered out.

Inside the enormous office there were books, and papers stacked in shambling towers that made it look like some madman was building a city. And maybe one was. Dr. Burrell continued his soft-spoken, yet unrelenting patter about Julian's uniqueness, scientific advancements, computer advancements, while also slipping in questions: had he ever heard of Moore's law? Julian admitted he hadn't. Dr. Burrell, shuffling his unruly stacks— miraculously-- without knocking over anything stopped in mid-patter to read something, deeply. Several long minutes passed. Just as Julian palmed a Xanax the doctor looked up and said, "Ok! among thousands of other advancements the discovery of a "luciferase-like" enzyme in mealworm larvae fits the bill as an intermediate between the luciferase enzyme that causes bioluminescence and enzymes that do not result in light. Researchers hope to modify the enzyme to alter both brightness and color." With a slight pivot of his body, he set the page on another stack, almost tenderly. Then he asked, Did Julian glow?

Julian pretended to clear his throat so he could slip the second Xanax into his mouth washing it down with the bottle of water he always carried with him because he could not swallow pills dry. After a few more minutes of hearing him talk, Julian understood the effectiveness of simple water drip torture. An hour after that, the doctor said the magic words, payment for his valuable participation, and being stoned, sad, and feeling it was all he had, he agreed to sell his sperm for great sums of money. And once he caught on to the potential profits his own body manufactured, he decided that curious doctors would no longer get free samples; there would be no more free cheek swabs, blood samples or skin scrapings. After that Julian went home to resume his self-destructive pattern of drinking, taking pills, and working on Naomi to find him a way to visit Grey in the hospital.

"I've offered the dear Mrs. Mars a pretty attractive admission fee, but she won't allow it. She knows it's all she has to torture you with. She can't torture Mars, so I guess you're *It*. And believe me that little woman is a big ball of fury in tiny high heels."

Julian listened to the call with one ear on the table, and the phone pressed against the other. The ocean roared. Naomi's voice was the wind pushing the waves into the sea.

"Thanks for trying Naomi," Julian said again.

"Julian, look, you do have other things to worry about. I know you got a cushion, but you're a young man, it's only going to last maybe twenty years. And working is better that what you are doing to yourself now. Have you thought about what we talked about?"

"Yes." He didn't tell her about the sperm sales.

"I can get you some work if you will just hear me out."

"A freak in a freak show?" Julian said bitterly, pulling at his skin.

"You work in *show biz*, so what kind of asinine comment is that? This is the ultimate freak show and you know it. And it pays well for it too." Naomi laughed. Julian laughed politely, just to show he got the joke.

Outside Julian mucked the soggy leaves out the old fountain. The fountain was stark-modern like the house, rough stack rocks, metal pour spouts, a copper lining in the catch basin. Because everyone who'd ever seen it thought he should love it, too, he'd gone through periods of trying to warm to it, but he couldn't. Growing up in a country like Norway, with beautiful, crystalline waters pouring over the thousands of natural falls forged by ancient geological activity, made all man-made fountains ruined saints.

Early that morning he'd had some sort of vision of Grey bathing naked in the basin he had just cleaned out. In this dream Grey was laughing, the hungry hyena laugh, like he did when he thought he had found love. "My water logs are still dry, Juli!" Grey had sang, "why the fuck aren't we on the river?" Julian felt like wood again, like when he had sat waiting for the bad news he knew was sure to come.

When water actually began pouring over the lip of the fountain, making tin music as it spilled, Julian had to run his hand under it to see if it was real. That it was, and that he had thought he was quite possibly hallucinating it, didn't strike Julian as warped thinking. He was too high. To celebrate it's success he took a shower in it, felt he was missing something so he got out, dripped back into the house to wash down more pills with a cold beer, before going back out again to lay under the pour over, overwhelmed with thoughts about all the crazy white water he'd crashed over with Grey Mars in his waterlogs.

Later that day, standing in his room stark naked trying to get his thoughts ordered enough to dress himself in dry clothes his

70

phone began ringing. Grey's names came up as the caller. He thought it was the terrible Mrs. Mars, calling to taunt him again, but he had to answer anyway, just in case.

"Juli, aren't you ever going to visit me?" Grey whispered weakly.

"Grey! She won't let me in," Julian whispered, gripping the phone like this would keep Mars there, alive.

"She's gone now."

"I'm on my way," Julian whispered back.

Pulling a wrinkled shirt from the top of the laundry basket, Julian drove to see Mars  wearing pajama bottoms, flip flops and a bright t-shit that advertised Sour Green Lime Tequila

.

# Chapter Eight

Even on his deathbed, Grey Mars was a pretty good actor. He convinced the Mrs. Mars how much he loved their house, and would do anything to keep it, so she took the house in lieu of a larger cash pay out, and a divorce agreement. Once she had packed and left, Mars decided he'd best get back to the real world. He explained this all to Julian using halting breaths. The man was still very weak, but he would live, Julian was certain.

"Well you move in with me," Julian told him.

"Just for awhile. Once I can get on alone I'll find a place in the hills near you. Juli good things are going to come. Can't you stop drinking and listen to Naomi. Take the work. Have a little faith in your fans? She'll protect you better than an army."

After that Julian talked to Naomi about the work she had found him.

"There are groups of people in Japan. You've become a source of great interest there. They want to talk to you about life as an actor, your film roles as Aqua Man, how you've adapted to being blue."

"I haven't adapted at all," Julian told Naomi.

"Okay so maybe you never will. Make some shit up. What do you want people to think they know about you? People like reassurance, a message of world peace. Especially the modern Japanese. They work themselves to death. Those people seem to think it's something you did on purpose, to become stronger or to elevate your soul or some *waa-waa*," Naomi said. "Also, they want you for some commercials. I'm sending an assistant who speaks fluent Japanese, Anise. Don't let the delicate flower name fool you either, she's an Amazon. She understands that culture, and will be your guiding light."

"My guiding light?" Julian asked.

"No booze, no pills, no nothing that isn't healthy. Start pumping up your physique. No one is going to exploit, harm or even touch you. No crazy game shows. No women, no sex. There are a lot out there that want your baby right now."

"Absurd," Julian insisted, staying mum about the sperm sales, deciding then and there that that particular epoch of stupidity was over, and a secret he would take to his grave as Mars always advised.

"Everyone has a good time and we all get paid. She'll see to your every need. There are some parties they'll pay you to attend, too. Take a tux. Listen, can you scuba dive?"

"Of course," Julian replied.

"Then take your wetsuit, too, I got something great lined up along those lines, too. Anise dives, too, so there'll be no bullshit going on there either. Julian, you can trust Anise, I want you to believe me on this. And give me a set of keys so I can move Grey Baby in while you're gone. I've got the nurses lined up, all male so no more of that heartbreak crap until he can get to it on his own. He's going to need a nurse twenty-four-seven, so I'll clear out a space they can use for breaks and rest. They tend to stay longer if they have a privacy room," she said, or rather ordered.

"There are three bedrooms, and the office. I'll clear out my room, you arrange the space however you have to." Julian began to worry that Naomi was the father he'd always longed to have. After he cleared out his bedroom for Mars, he began lifting weights, ordered better food and packed that evening.

Anise was a six-foot tall, blonde force with a to-do list written by Naomi. She actually had two cell phones. "For my mother," she explained waving one. "I gotta be able to turn her off. I even had a special app built that answers her calls and gives her a long rambling rundown of my life. I record them before I go to bed. The app leaves space for her to admonish me. I never play it back."

Julian thought she may be already speaking Japanese, but for the entire trip she managed to deflect everyone with a forceful finesse. Julian felt freer leaving his house than he had in months.

Tokyo was so brilliant he could not take his eyes off of it. They were walking, at his request, to the hotel. The bags were sent ahead, Anise was his only bodyguard. Julian slowed down, trying to get the larger picture of all he was seeing broken down into the smaller, defined parts. The odor of fish did not surprise him, but the order and cleanliness did. After the second time of her striding away without realizing Julian had stopped to look something over: the view, a group of people, a storefront with things for sale that he could not imagine the purpose for, she stopped, wrote out something in Japanese and stuffed it into his top pocket.

"Don't lose that. If we somehow get separated, hand that to anyone and they will take you right to the hotel. You can feel safe going with them. Or hail a taxi. No one speaks English here, just so you know. Give me your hand," she ordered. After that Anise led him around holding his hand like a leash, her grip man-strong. The paper would never be used; she had no intention of losing track of Julian again. He did not intend to pull away.

The Japanese were a perplexing people to Julian. Extremely health conscious, with vending machines that sold juice, real fruit, but mostly this milky tea drink he could not appreciate when Anise stopped and bought them both one. "I dream about this stuff," she sighed, sipping it down. Julian carried his in his free hand until he could discreetly drop it into a waste can. The machines didn't seem to dispense soft drinks. Many people smoked cigarettes like it was oxygen of the gods. "They love Jack Daniels, well any and all types of whiskey," Anise commented after Julian's comment.

"Let's go in and have a drink. I'd like to see how they behave in bars," he teased.

"No bars," she said steering him away. "Naomi has both of us on booze lockdown."

Julian did not crave alcohol. This was the least of what he wanted, he thought, studying Anise who was talking on the phone, after she parked Julian on a bench and stood guard in front of him. He people-watched while she made arrangements.

The children were bundled up and obviously carefully tended to. Certain females who passed by presented themselves as modest, almost to the point of blushing under behind their hands, when he smiled and waved at them, but wore things like skirts that were printed with pictures that looked like their panties were showing through. Another group walked by carrying attractive suitcases.

"Airline hostesses?" Julian asked Anise.

"Those *Hirojuku* girls are mostly in Tokyo. The girls carry suitcases so they can change their outfits before they go home. They wear American looks in the city but, of course, no cleavage or backs are shown. They are more like what we would call *cuter,* not in the teenage fashion sense, but in the ruffles, feminine look, they are fad conscious, but it's between them. Believe me they spend as more time planning those outfits then they do wearing them." Anise said.

Julian badly wanted to point out that they had no cleavage and most of their backs were about the width of his hand, making either very difficult to catch so much as a glimpse of even if they were strutting around naked. He kept it to himself while Anise went back to another phone call. Julian brought out his guidebook, and read over a few pages.

It seemed that all around was some of the best hiking, skiing, scuba diving in the world, but they spent most of their time doing similar activities indoors. This information he shared with Anise.

"Put the book down and look at the real place. They go for walks and fish outdoors. Mainly they are a very unhappy people. They work themselves to death. It's called *karoshi.* They can build anything, but they have no knack for enjoying it, taking a break. That's why you are here. They are always trying to find that magic door," Anise said. After that, he surrendered the book and let her take the lead.

A group of teen girls passed by wearing bizarre get-ups that seemed like punk rock, meets apple blossom festival's furry little creatures. "Those are the *Hirojuku* girls," Anise said like that explained them sufficiently.

Everyone stared at him, but few reached out to touch him. "It's not impolite to stare at us," Anise said. "We both look foreign. It's a novelty, like appreciating a work of art. It's flattering."

Julian knew why people stared, and for once, he didn't mind. The truth was, he was staring, too. Norway was a homogenous country, but this was mainly of social beliefs, there was variation in hair and eye color there, not like America, of course. In Japan there didn't seem to be. Everyone had dark hair and eyes, it was impossible not to study the way they looked and moved. People approached him, and unlike in America, Julian was not afraid of being spit on, or shot. They seemed to want to pet him.

It was truly hilarious when someone got too close, and Anise flashed her liquid blue eyes, and broke out her fluent Japanese whenever someone got too close, she commanded them back, probably reminding them of their place. They reeled back, with many bringing out cameras to snap a shot, obviously as much entertained by this turn of events as they were startled. Anise and Julian seemed to be providing comic relief. He liked that.

"Smile. They realize you are someone famous even if they don't know who you are yet. Maybe we'll get an extra job or two out of this." Another person wandered toward Julian, Anise flavored the air with her rapid Japanese, making the crowd both laugh and close in. After that it became a game with several innings before Anise decided it was time to move on.

"Okay, they know your name now," Anise assured him.

"Maybe I should hire you," Julian said. Anise smiled broadly at this. A zip of pleasure shivered in his gut.

After a few minutes he wanted to prolong the experience of walking outdoors, feeling such freedom. He was certain he could crumble to the ground with his wallet wide open and no one would touch a thing, and then as if to prove his hypothesis, they turned a corner and there was a guy passed out in middle of the sidewalk with wallet half out of his back pocket, while people just walked around him quietly ignoring him. He wished Grey Mars were there to take it all in. Those sardonic opinions and insights would be a welcome bridge from his limited culture to this mysterious place. Why had Julian never come before?

"Is there something going on?" Julian asked when they came across a large group of theatrically dressed teens in bizarre costumes.

"It's Animae, from animated cartoons that are popular here," Anise said like that explained it. "Like if you dressed up as your favorite cartoon character, say Casper, the Friendly Ghost." She was kidding of course, but he had no idea who she was referencing. Julian didn't watch television as a child, he played outside even in winter, but he didn't pursue it; just felt relieved he didn't have kids and their fads to adjust around.

"You can't blame the kids for wanting to get a close look. Getting a picture with you will make their day, especially these young teens," she counseled Julian. "Your skin is just so exotic and beautiful. So many people want it now."

Julian murmured something polite because he didn't know what to say. No one wanted to be blue, having lived it, he was certain. But, when she waved him in for a picture he went with a warm smile.

76

"And don't let their delicate appearance fool you. Their DNA is warlords, and Shogun," she said with some pride. Julian always flinched at the acronym, DNA, feeling so betrayed by his own he couldn't forgive any of it. This led to thoughts on the sperm he so freely sold, but when he brought up a hand to work his nails against his teeth, Anise took it gently down.

"Growing up here, I do admit I used to wish to be so utterly, delicately tiny and pretty."

"You have true beauty, that is so much more than *pretty*," Julian said.

"Hey thanks Julian," Anise said, her smile radiated as only a twenty-three year olds does when a compliment hits them square in the heart.

People spoke to him like he belonged, even if he could not understand them, he had to give them that. Anise faithfully translated when she thought she should. "It takes so long," she explained, "because there is so much razzle-dazzle you have to start with before you can say anything sufficiently vague enough not to cross any lines." She sighed deeply, the first indication that Japan was, of course, more taxing for her than for him. Especially with him. He was glad to be able to skim over the surface.

"Japanese is both difficult and easy. Easy in that it's a language of extremely regular structure, difficult in that it's completely unlike English. A person can learn Japanese when he abandons pretty much every notion of how language is "supposed" to work. You don't need it though. Naomi said you speak several languages. She said you got her neighbor's cat out of the tree by speaking its first language to it, like what was it, Norwegian? Spanish? French? My dogs speak Japanese."

"Yes," he said without elaborating. All of his life he'd had an extremely good ear for language, but the Japanese language seemed so impenetrable, so mystifying Julian found he completely ignored it. His defense against it and culture shock was Anise, his assistant, his beautiful, strong shield. They went to several parties, and some shopping junkets, all carefully planned, even down to what he bought, before the first lecture.

After their first day, they became some kind of power couple on the Japanese circuit. After the first lecture, which Julian thought of as a story telling hour, with another hour and a half given over to questions, all translated by Anise. Julian was sad that he was not as deep and soulful as they probably wanted him to be. It just wasn't easy being blue. After that they went to a party he'd agreed to attend. The money they paid him to sit and talk over martinis astonished him, but Naomi arranged it, and to make Mars happy Julian went. Later in the week they shot commercials for whiskey, and a blue moon saki, and underwear in the mornings, in which he struck Rodin like poses. That evening he went to give another lecture about the Amazon jungle and turning blue, and afterward a party, where Julian told the story of getting chased out by tiny dark natives waving sharp axes that looked alarmingly modern. This was before Julian turned blue, he explained. They all laughed as Anise translated, so he more or less left it all in her hands.

"From their questions I think they seem to think I'm going to become immortal," Julian said to Anise. They traveled by a small, chauffeured car everywhere they went. The size meant they spent much time wedged together with Julian breathing in her scent as he brushed away strands of her long hair.

"They think you drank mercury and lived and now you're immortal, like some ancient Lord. They loved your movies. You are so beautiful, different, but a perfectly symmetrical human, truly a work of art. All things appreciated by the Japanese," Anise said.

They were hanging at the door of his hotel room. The first time she had gone in his room to make sure everything was as promised, but then she'd kept to the perimeters and they didn't make eye contact while she was in the room. Anise had left saying, "call me if you need anything," by way of a quick, polite goodbye. They'd been inching closer now, a few words from across the hall to lingering in the middle to leaning against a wall, dragging out the last few thoughts about the long, long day. By now the good byes were getting longer, their noses were now almost touching.

"Does your toilet play beautiful sounds when you flush it?" Julian asked, stalling.

"Naomi says I can't sleep with you," Anise sighed. He'd heard her say this probably a dozen times now. His usual answer was ready.

"It's best. I find these days I get seriously depressed after spending time with a good woman. I mean it'll probably happen anyway, it did after Rini, and there was nothing sexual in that friendship."

"You mean after your own father shot you?"

Julian nodded. Anise blinked, "Well Mr. Mars will be there with you now. He's great company. You'll probably have to keep him sedated to keep him down though. He's a cannonball." She kissed him, but when he leaned in she pulled back, considering something.

"I have a boyfriend. He might propose any day," she said.

"Anise, you are too young to marry," Julian said.

"I want kids."

For Julian the moment was completely lost.

"I guess I could always just buy sperm when I'm ready," she said.

There was that again, Julian thought uncomfortably. Sliding the key out of his pocket and opened the door.

"Where are you going?" she asked.

*I'm exhausted. I know what it feels like to drown*, Julian wanted to say, but by then they were already kissing hard.

# Chapter Nine

After Japan, he came home ready to face whatever came next, sober, and single, but with directed purpose, well wherever either Naomi or Mars directed. At the airport, Anise begged him to keep "everything a secret."

"You have my word," Julian said, relieved. They never again saw each other face-to-face, but she was a prolific with sending thoughtful texts, and charming emails meant to let Julian down with ease, he thought. This made him like her more, but never enough to call her. There was no chance he would ever tell anyone.

His house awakened again with the noise and color of recovering Grey Mars. An army brat, Mars knew something about Japan, and he was ready to talk about it.

"Juli, I saw the commercials, and I read they loved you over there. I think it's time we started expanding on this blue skin thing more. Right?" His growing energy fairly rumbled from his chest, but hadn't made it to his voice, but Julian was no longer afraid Mars would die, not even secretly in a small corner of his darkest, most fearful thoughts.

"I do have that screen play I've been waiting to show you."

Mars's hyena laugh wheezed, and skittered, but it still pulled from the soles of his feet.

"You ever hear from your old man again?"

"When I got home, he called several times a day. I just couldn't pick up. Lately he has started calling constantly again. Someone must have shown him the Japanese commercials," Julian admitted.

"Yeah. Well. I don't know what to say. You don't think he'd travel here do you?"

"No. Never," Julian answered. He thought about the last long message his father had left, according to the timer on the machine over nine minutes. Julian erased it without listening to any part of it, and this bothered him, he couldn't help the weakness.

"Before I forget. I just want to give you fair warning. Some people are stopping by, Juli." Mars informed him of visitors this every morning. There was never a day when Mars could be without some type of audience.

Little by little Julian was beginning to relax around Mars's people. He still avoided mirrors, but he began to look forward to the small parties Grey would get to come sit around his bed, telling tales, making deals, mercilessly ripping apart books and movies over ice coffee, an odd new addiction of his after he claimed he could not stand it hot. Because of his medicines, and physical therapy, Mars could not drink alcohol, and because of his growing problem with it, Julian wouldn't either.

"The rags are reporting that I'm close to death. Having seizures," Grey said one morning. His eyebrows dug at each other. "Why seizures?" He asked the ceiling.

Julian had to fake much of his laugh, but after Grey swatted his knee with the paper, it all seemed to settle down, and they were able to have a normal conversation.

One morning a UCLA student called to request a serious interview with Julian. UCLA was both their alma mater and where his career started along with his friendship with Grey Mars. During the interview he did his best to be straight forward, and answer her questions about turning blue as best he could without sounding like he was resigned to it. He liked the article after he read it. She had kindly focused on his accomplishments. There was no mention of his recent gunshot wound in Norway although he told her some of the story, so he could explain how Grey Mars had saved his life. More than anything he wanted her to understand that crass seeming Mars was a true great friend in the best sense.

"Bright kid, but she missed the obvious subtleties about you, Juli," Mars said seriously, tossing the paper in disappointment. Julian told him he thought that it was fine. After that Naomi called to tell Julian that the Discovery Channel contacted her to see if he would narrate a series on mutations and adaptations that would include a look at the blue lobster, and his transformation. Julian told her he couldn't think of a project he would enjoy more, as long as no one served him the blue lobster to eat.

Mars improved, but it wasn't rapid and a year later he still had a limp; his vision had changed enough that he now wore glasses. Julian watched in awe as his friend bought two dozen pair, like others bought shoes. Once he was up and going well enough they got busy. Together they made two successful sci-fi movies, films they were both proud of. Julian starred. But during the filming of the second one there were a few days that Julian was made up (actually every part of him was carefully air brushed painted) to look like his natural, before the blue, color, that pale Norwegian flesh tone of those most naïve, conceited days.

"There you go, your alter ego," the tactful make up artist had said with her finishing touch. The process had taken hours to turn every part of him flesh colored again.

The mirror reflected someone he no longer recognized. Like Narcissus, he found it impossible to stop looking in the mirror. Several times he found himself rubbing at his arm until the blue came through. This was like spotting a shiny dime on the ground, but when he reached for it the shock of finding an oil slick, but this was even more terrible.

This regression to progression as he'd come to think of it over the days he had to become his natural color again left Julian feeling more limited and restless. The life he had always imagined as an actor was never to be, he finally accepted that. It had taken years, but he finally accepted that. Once the movie wrapped, and all the gifts had been given and the cast photos had been taken, Julian secretly – in his mind at least – resigned as an actor. His next big project would be trying to find his new purpose in life, something that would contribute to the world in some way: *Blue Man cracks terrorist code, saves country.*

One blazing hot summer morning Julian, drying off from a swim, found Naomi, Grey and two other strange men in the living room. The strangers were obviously startled by Julian, and instead of responding to his nod they stared at him.

"Why are you blue?" One of them finally asked. He knew that accent right away.

"Why are you sitting in my living room?" Julian replied gesturing toward the front door.

"Juli, sit down. There is some serious news," Grey said.

A dozen disasters flashed through his mind, but he felt he'd already been through the worst, what could possibly be left? Grey was there and alive. Julian braced himself, but he was not prepared when Grey said, "These men have come to tell you that your father is gone."

"Gone?" Julian inquired, baffled. All of his life his father had been gone.

"Take it easy Juli, just let it sink in," Grey said.

"He's conveyed to you many millions of dollars," one of the men said quickly.

"Conveyed?" Julian repeated. "Millions of dollars? How many millions?"

"Many, many millions. You are quite rich now."

Julian sank into the chair Mars pointed to. He knew his father with all his black market, underhanded deals made a comfortable living, and the old man was alive during two wars, but this! All his life he had attended good boarding schools, and since he was twelve, one in the United States, which his father had paid for, not really knowing where he was. The cost was something he never complained about, although it was the equivalent to an average annual salary. But when Julian wanted to go to the University of California, in Los Angeles, his father had refused to pay the tuition. Norway had the finest university education in the world, he'd said stubbornly, and it was free. It was only through three months of work on Julian's part did he find an eager engineering student willing to switch places with him -- this wasn't unheard of -- but the arrangements were difficult, and left every year a challenge just to meet the costs. On graduation day, he'd felt the better man for it, but was always certain this was not the point his father was trying to make. Julian had always believed his proud father just could not afford it, but would never admit to that. Strangely, that obviously was not true.

"Here, here!" Naomi cried, flagging a hand trying to wave Julian back into the present.

"Grey Mars, it seems we are free to do what we want now," Julian said.

The Mars hyena came out full blast, startling both the strange men to their feet.

"Sit down," Grey commanded them. "Have a drink, and bring out all the papers so we can give them a good look over."

Once he was satisfied that it was not a hoax, Julian went to dust off the bottle of champagne, to see what he had left in the bar, and grab some glasses, but he was thinking that he wanted to try his hand at photography, to find a purpose, build a better house, and he wanted to read everything. The celebration was low key, but also an odd mix of disbelief and then relief kept spiraling through him. Julian hoped the ghost of his father would stay gone in Norway for the rest of his life, but he did not believe for a minute that his father was dead.

# Chapter Ten

Five years later.

      One bright morning when Julian was heading out for his now daily run, just past his driveway some kind of paper stuck to the sole of his shoe. The paper turned out to be a 'Homes of the Stars' map. Julian was surprised to see his home noted accurately as "the Blue Man's house" on that very street. No one ever bothered him anymore, although he was writing, everything he published or sold was under a pseudonym, he never worked as an actor, or made any public appearances. He'd never seen a tour bus on his narrow street, but he didn't care if they went by or not. Julian had come to a point where he refused to notice the outside world. To help reduce litter in his lovely neighborhood, he folded the map and stuck it into his shorts pocket and finished his run. After that he went to lift some weights, check in with Mars on a project they were developing, and work on his latest painting, which was so terrible he could not give up on it. These days he felt incredibly good, as long as he kept his mind off being blue, and the kaleidoscope of everything else that had become his rather thin past. In all these years Julian had taught himself to be very narrow-minded, but it was something he had always done to keep the unwanted thoughts out.

      When the doorbell rang, Julian clicked on the computer to see who was at his front gate. He was astonished to see a woman with a big straw hat holding the hand of a blonde child with skin as blue as his own. The calendar said Halloween was weeks away, so he sighed deeply and went back to his book. The bell persisted and then one of the gardeners called, "Senor Azul tu hija esta!"

      That got Julian out of his chair to look at the monitor again. He didn't have a daughter. There was the woman fishing in her purse, while the little girl stood rod straight, facing the gate expectantly. After another few minutes her head dropped, her shoulders slumped. Then it came to Julian how a blue daughter of his might be actually standing at his gate.

      "I'm coming," he said through the speaker making the little girl jump back and then tip her face to the sky, smiling.

"How can I help you?" Julian asked the pair, as soon as he opened the gate.

"I think you're my dad," the little girl said, putting her hand—her blue hand—on his matching blue hand as confirmation.

Julian looked at the other woman whose smile barely etched her face, her eyes darting uncertainly from the girl to Julian, and back to the girl, like she was ready to grab her and run depending on how this went. Before Julian could think of what to say, she stood in front of the little blue girl.

"Her momma bought the, uh, stuff, to get, well a baby started. She was going through a liberal period, entered some study. Anyway, she's blue, you're blue. Your DNA, half her DNA, your gnomes are all over the Internet. It was easy to get a match done. And you are on the Map of the Stars so it was easy to locate your house, too."

"I beg your pardon?" Julian asked, confused.

"My little granddaughter here has hit a rough patch. There's a stepfather now. He wants her to go to boarding school, or live with me. Of course she can live with me, I would never let her go live alone. She's seven years old! Can you imagine?"

Yes, he said, he certainly knew the devastation of boarding school for a seven year old. "Come in," Julian said holding the gate open.

"Someone brought you to her attention, and so well, here we are," she gave a *can you blame her?* shrug.

"And what is your name little miss?" he asked, taking her hand back into his.

"Sky Blue," she said. Her eyes slid up to his warily. "Do you like it?"

"I wouldn't want any other name for you," Julian said. She let out a sigh of relief, and then began to tell Julian the name of every stuffed toy she owned, which seemed somewhere around one hundred, and the plot to her favorite book, and something about her little dog. After that she demonstrated how her dog barked at her new stepfather every time he came in, this made them both laugh, though Julian barely understood a word she said, he knew how to fake a comradely laugh, who in Hollywood didn't?

"You remind me someone." Of course Julian was thinking of Mars.

86

"Is that a good thing?" Sky asked, again looking at him nervously.

"As long as you stay out of the vodka," Julian said, smiling.

"I have no idea what that means, but of course I will," Sky said.

Julian turned to the grandmother and asked, "What do you expect from me?"

The woman smiled at Julian. "You're blue, she's blue. She needs someone her own color. It's clear you're her father whether you wanted it to turn out this way or not. They promised her mother the child would not be blue. We don't need money, if that's what you mean. I live in Brentwood."

Sky folded her arms across her chest, pulling herself inside her own wings, how well Julian knew that feeling.

"Sky, what would you like me to do?" Julian asked.

"We could go places. Be each other's blue friend. I can read to you," she said.

"If your grandmother will come too, I can do that," Julian said although he wasn't all that certain he could. For the past few years he bordered on being an agoraphobic, and he knew nothing about little girls. He spent his childhood in all boys' boarding schools or on an isolated farm alone with a cook, his mother a ghost—Julian blocked it out.

"I can call you Sir," Sky said. "You should call me Blue Dot."

"Blue Dot?"

"Blue for my skin, and dot is short for daughter."

"Sky, I think we should use our real names."

Sky said, "Can I have some water?"

Julian told her he could use some himself, before he turned to her grandmother and asked her if he could get her anything.

"I wouldn't mind getting into that vodka a little bit," she replied genially.

"I'll see to the drinks," Julian said.

"I'll go with you," Sky said following him.

Looking down at the top of Sky's head, her blue part in the blonde scalp, Julian had to refrain himself from placing his hand on the top of it, as he had watched the grandmother do time and again.

They sat inside in the living room making awkward conversation until Cloris stated that they were leaving before they broke the rules of civility. When it was time for them to go Julian stood at the door watching them make their way to the gate. The little girl, Sky was a strange creature, pretty, polite and astonishingly cheerful. He could not believe he could have had anything to do with creating anything so fine. Julian thought his avoidance of children had come from childhood experiences with other lonely, unhappy boarding school kids trying to keep themselves in one piece. This left him humming an old nursery tune, oddly enough.

Later, when Mars dropped by for their weekly business discussion Julian told him the story to Mars's utter delight. The hyena laughed again and again, a pack of them gorging on the story.

"Did you ever read anything about a blue girl?" Julian asked him.

"Dismissed it as another crap hoax story. There have been many stories, but you know, who would believe that bullshit? Maybe I should be paying closer attention to things. Whose kid is it?" Mars said.

Julian decided to tell Mars about the crazy epoch of drug haze and bizarre sperm and blood donation. He had to confess he didn't know how much, but he was sure daily for maybe a month. For a second Mars went pale, but as usual his face contorted, his elbows flapped and then everything went back to normal. "You getting involved with your daughter?" he asked.

"I promised to take her to Disneyland. You ever been there?" Julian asked.

"No, but I'll get you a bodyguard," Mars said. "Any where they call the happiest place on earth is going to be full of unhappy people disappointed that nothing changes even with polished cheerful colors everywhere."

"The grandmother is coming, too." Julian sighed, lost again about his role in the world, but when he looked to Mars for guidance, his friend only shrugged.

"I haven't a clue," he said, this time chuckling. "But, I think this will be good for you."

The next time they came over, he was better prepared with foods the grandmother said Sky preferred when they had talked on the phone. The minute they arrived Julian resolved to study everything about the way the grandmother parented Sky so he had some sort of road map to follow.

"So I spread the peanut butter on the bread, and then on top of that this jelly," Julian asked. They were in his kitchen, working side by side while her grandmother, Cloris, sipped a coffee. Sky volunteered to make the first sandwich, this PBJ, and in her usual congenial manner asked Julian if he'd like one.

"I'm not sure. I've never eaten peanut butter before. Norwegian children eat chocolate on their buttered bread." Julian said hoping this was not about to lead to a long drawn out explanation of the cacao versus the peanut plant. Sky was a kid that liked to know everything if she asked about it. This often scared the wits out of Julian. He wasn't used to this much conversation.

"So is my other grandmother Norwegian?"

At first Julian didn't know who she meant.

"Your mother," Cloris nudged in her quiet, shepherding way that was her style.

"My mother," Julian said weakly, catching his breath, he thought about what he might say. "Your Norwegian grandmother was very religious, full of old fashioned, uh, beliefs, and ideas. Superstitions, I suppose. When I was seven years old she took me to live at school. I think I told you that I always lived at school as a child. But after that time, I never saw her again."

"She left you alone?" Sky's eyes filled with tears.

Julian frantically added, "No I had the cook and my fa-- father. Later when I was eleven, I had a roommate that was an American. After that I knew where I wanted to live so I registered myself to a school in America and the next year, I left Norway."

The tears spilled out, flowing down her cheeks, and when he looked to Cloris for a rescue she was wiping her eyes, too. Sky stood frozen for a few minutes, and when she looked back at him she was smiling.

"So your mother became a fairy and flew off into the magic forest where she can feel happy. Did you know every time a baby laughs another fairy gets her wings?"

"Pardon?" Julian said, not really making any sense out of that, but also thinking his mother would approve.

"Whatever your favorite color is, her fairy costume is probably that color. Maybe it's blue. Maybe she buzzes around to check on you still. Even though you are grown." Sky nodded satisfied. She dried her eyes on the back of her hand and smiled. Cloris shrugged, and sipped her coffee. Julian was desperate to know how Sky could make that shift, like Mars, there was always a pathway out of the storm and into the sunlight.

At Disneyland, he was so nervous he kept dropping his keys once they all got out of the van. Grey came along cheerfully bringing an enormous bodyguard that Julian had known from his acting days. The glistening, pastel iced, and gold gilded place frightened him, but Sky jumped up and down and clapped her hands. Cloris quietly admonished Sky to settle down, but she was smiling at the place, too, and her feet seemed to be running in place, like she couldn't wait to get in there either. Julian felt a tad bit betrayed by everyone. He desperately needed water.

"You sure *this* is the place you want to go?" He asked Sky seriously, causing Grey Mars to let out the pack of hungry hyenas. Sky took his hand.

"You're going to love this," she assured him. Julian let her pull him along.

The day went as tensely as Julian had feared. People stared and pointed, something Sky was able to ignore completely. He was puzzled by the zeal with which people wore mouse ears. Even Mars had a pair on a black cap embroidered with his name on it. This was where Julian drew the line in indulging Sky, absolutely no mouse ears were going on his head. And there was never a time when he would agree to advertise for any company for free. Sky, Grey, Cloris, even the bodyguard could leave with whatever they wanted, Julian was going out dressed exactly the way he came in, nervously jingling the keys in his pocket. Many people stopped him for his autograph, it surprised Julian and also made him nervous for Sky. He signed the various scraps of paper and napkins with *Julian, the Blue Man*. Many pictures were taken, every shutter click making him inwardly cringe. He did not want Sky dragged into the fray, but now knew she would be.

"We're like the only blue people in the world, except for Smurfs," Sky observed.

"Smurfs?" Julian asked, hopefully. Sky told him the entire plot to what he thought might be some demented cartoon feature originating from his homeland.

"If you had a beard you could be Papa Smurf," she concluded, studying him with her usual searching stare.

"I'm not growing a beard, Miss Sky Blue Dot," Julian said.

The long, long day went approximately as he had predicted. There was one very tense tête-à-tête that occurred between the Disney security and Julian's bodyguard, when a boy got too close to Sky and informed her she was blue, and weird, and ugly. The bodyguard put his hand extremely close to the kid's face and by suggestion only, pushed him away while shielding Sky.

"Kids don't like my blue skin," she said like it was something she had come to realize and accept, something Julian still could not do, not really. He also knew she never would either, not completely. Being an outsider was probably a leading cause of insanity. In that moment, he wanted to give her everything, wondering if a diamond necklace would somehow take out some of the sting. If not, what would do for a small girl possessed of so much goodness, and innocence?

Grey Mars and Sky moderated the incident to everyone's satisfaction, though Julian secretly hoped they would be ejected from the park. Of course they weren't. They might be blue, but Julian's wealth was now well known. Disney assigned a small team to accompany them the rest of their stay. They were first in every line. During the fireworks when Sky fell asleep against Julian with a thud he took this as his get away opportunity, gathered her up in his arms and carried her back to the safety of the warm van, and home.

They talked about it over their next lunch together. The day was sunny and they went out to the pool to eat. Sky bubbled over about Disneyland, and tried to convince Julian that he shouldn't worry about her.

"I guess we have to be the two blue people in the world," he said as some kind of pathetic conciliation. He did not know how to comfort her. Look at the mess he made of his life, he lacked the emotional resources, but it didn't mean he would give up trying for her life, though he could only imagine what she was in store for.

Of course, once the pictures hit the news, other blue children appeared, much to the delight of Sky. Julian had actually got her the thing she most desired, other blue friends. Actually half brothers and sisters, when they first started arriving she clapped her hands with joy. After about a month of the visitors, Sky's eye began to narrow when they sidled too close to Julian and she began to experience what all first-born children do when a new sibling is born.

"They all know you're my dad, right?" She asked Julian.

Julian patted her shoulder, the way her grandmother did when she wanted Sky to settle down and stop chattering, but this did not calm her at all. The tears were forming bubbles in her lower lids.

"You are my one and only," Julian told her. This seemed to satisfy Sky.

For Julian almost every day was a new barrage of blue children showing up to meet him, brought alone by their mothers, fathers, aunts, uncles, and others. These were rather awkward interviews. So far no one had asked him for anything. All of the encounters left him frazzled, and something like angry. When he sold the sperm, and maybe he had been too stoned, or over wrought over Grey Mars, or too naively idiotic to really put it all together, but he had never really made the connection that it would be used to start actual, human babies that would be his real children.

The caregivers of his blue progeny usually had the same to offer to Julian: "There are so many challenges, but I am just so grateful to have my beautiful, smart child, with such excellent health. We were told about your blue skin, but the doctors assured all of us it would drown in the fierce white genetic pool— white being the default color in all apes, according to them-- making his offspring *secretly* superior. The human race would become fortified by his genetic contribution, they were supremely confident. Now the blueness makes them all the more special, I don't have to tell you, do I?"

"I find it very difficult to be blue," Julian said honestly. "The child will have challenges."

92

Often the women, the mother's to be specific, would tell him how astonished they were that he would go along with such a thing. There was nothing astonishing about his part in all of this, jerking off was easy. No, it was harnessing all the wombs of all of those otherwise brilliant women to implant them with so many radical embryos.

The human race was supposed to become fortified by his genetic contribution, they were supremely confident. So that was the hook to get all these smarty-pants to line up and take the microscopic sperm into their bodies to nurture into a human for the good of all mankind. At that time, there was nothing so noble in his actions. Someone wanted him for something, it was that simple. Biologically, sperm was no trouble at all to produce, and it always seemed so completely disposable. It really never occurred to Julian that he could be actually fathering live humans. This surprised him still, and would for the rest of his long life.

Sometimes they asked him for money, his response was a direct order from Mars: *have your attorney contact my attorney*. They had signed away their rights to child support from him. As donor he was to forever remain anonymous. Well, since he couldn't they often thought the other agreements were flexible as well. They weren't. Julian was a generous man, but he would decide what he would give, to whom and when. His board of directors was composed of Mars, Naomi, Rini, and even Cloris if she was willing to weigh in. Occasionally he sent Talia secret gifts, it kept him from driving there to see her.

Even with Mars there, or sometimes Naomi as a buffer, the meetings were exhausting. After each left, and with the exception of Sky, he was more convinced he needed to get back into his cave to get away from them. His new cave would be at an anonymous location, and comfortable cave with enough room for everyone he loved. What haunted Julian most was how to do the right thing. He never wanted children because he never wanted to fail as a father. And now all these blue children—his—were out there in need of a steady hand. Julian found himself short of anything like a steady hand to offer.

One night he felt so overwhelmed he built a cave on his bed with an extra blanket and all the spare pillows he could find. It was hot inside, he had to bring in a fan, but it worked. As he finally drifted off to sleep entering that world of reality as his mind was dragged away to other depths before finally releasing him to full sleep.

That night Julian awoke to his father's voice ordering him to get out of the bed at once. *"Kom hjem nå, sønn." Come home now son*, he ordered.

When he opened his eyes he saw the outline of his father in the doorframe. "I am home. You go home," Julian said, intending to get up and vanish the image by waving his hands into it, but he found he couldn't move.

*"Kom hjem nå, sønn,"* the old man repeated. He held a closed fist out to Julian, opening it slowly to reveal an apple crushed to a gruesome sauce of seeds and apple pulp already rusting from the air.

Before Julian could move, his mother's specter appeared, hovering over his father, her white hand placed on the top of his head, an open palm pressing him to the floor until he became a tiny, single blob. She scooped it up, showing him the whole, perfect red apple.

*"Du er trygg nå, sønn,"* she said, eating the apple with her gleaming white teeth. *You are safe now, son*. Her long hair was down, blending into her nightgown, the edges glancing off the floor.

"Where is he really?" He asked his mother.

"Feeding the fish at the bottom of the sea where he came from. Now sleep. I am proud of you. You look so beautiful blue," she whispered.

Julian fell back into the pillow. During his next segment of sleep he smelled his mother's bread baking in the kitchen. Out his window was the luminous full moon, with the rabbit frozen in it. Throwing back the covers he hurried into the kitchen, but found it empty. Spotless. When he looked out the window, his body pressed against it to see high enough into the heavens, there was the moon, a fingernail clipping of pale white against the deep night sky. Julian went to the living room, tipping the couch over he climbed inside the cave and waited for morning to come. When he awoke, he was in bed, in his own room. The chairs had been repositioned, the water glass knocked over, and he didn't know what else. Julian went to his computer, opened a window to the moon phases that month. Last night had been a hidden moon-- the new moon, so nothing in the sky. The smell of his mother's baking bread still lingered in the air, edible.

In the late afternoon he was trying to review a script Mars had asked him to look over. Still shaken, he wanted to tell him, but couldn't bring himself to mention the dream, or the sleepwalking, or whatever it had been, to Grey Mars when he brought over lunch. Mars already believed Julian need a therapist. Maybe he did, he thought, but he wished he had told his mother that she had meant the world to him. He believed she had visited him, saved him. That first summer he had come home from school to find her gone, he had been told that she had abandoned him. Nothing more was to be said on the subject. Now he wondered if his father had murdered her. This was not something he could conceive of, and yet, of course he could. That house was still full of her things as long as he had kept going home he found them there, even her dresses were still in the closet, her hair combs on the dresser, her boots lined up against the wall of the back mud porch. The old farmhouse was probably still full of her things today, now that he thought about it. The place was in the list of his inheritance. Julian set the pages on the desk, used his closed fist on top for a paperweight, then a hammer pounding it flat. He couldn't work. And he couldn't think about this any more.

Julian moved to the smallest corner of his house so he could hear the newly worked fountain play its tune. At Sky's suggestion they had found an artist to rework the copper pan and the edge the water poured off so it played a kind of tinkling music when the water surged and fell. Usually it reminded him too much of the awful wind chimes sold in the garden shops so he kept it off unless Sky was visiting. That morning he turned it on, to settle his nerves, as if she was coming, but knew she had a dentist appointment. Seated near the smallest window in the house, alone, the house felt overwhelmingly claustrophobic. The open book lay in his lap. Julian, determined to make sense of certain classics he had always lied about reading, was now trying once again to crack Homer's, *The Odyssey*. He dug back in because he believed that somehow this story would give him some essential human wisdom on how to proceed with his life. Half a page in, he again lifted his head.

"Would it kill the *whoevers* in charge of this stuff, to write a version in a modern, comprehensible English?" He asked the jacket, reading over the translator's name as if this would help the words to penetrate. After that he flipped the pages, stopping at the words, "*afterwards a man finds pleasure in his pains, when he has suffered long and wandered long.*"

No, Julian thought. No! That is not what I want. I have to find something more than pain from this blue skin. After flinging the book, Julian dropped his face into his hands and sobbed, not for himself, but for Sky and the other blue children, his children that he stupidly created and sentenced to this life of outsider. What had he done? All the dithering on the new place was now over. He decided he would construct a place large enough for all the blue children to escape to, when they needed a breather from the earthy flesh toned world. In his mind he was thinking tennis court, swimming pool, bowling, ice skating rink, plush bedrooms, and a computer lab.

Julian called his friend the nurse, Rini, who has become his analyst, confident, wise interpreter of his dreams, and maladies.

"No matter the color, we are all made of the same star dust, Julian," Rini counseled, her image jittery because she liked to use her hands a lot in the Skype window. The cross he had given her caught a ray of light and twinkled like a star. He smiled, without Sky being there to cause it.

Julian told her about his dream, the apple, parents, the unmistakable scent of baking bread.

"She has probably been sending you signs for years, Julian," Rini replied confidentially. "You've been trying to ignore them, yes?"

Julian shook his head as he said, "probably. I think she may still be in the old house, somehow."

Rini shook her head. "You must never go there again. Leave it be," she advised seriously. Julian nodded.

"Please come visit," Julian ended every phone call this way.

"Yes. I think I will now. My children are independent. I would welcome the visit. I want to meet your daughter, Sky, and Cloris and of course the infamous Grey Mars who I'm afraid I picture as a cartoon character every time you say his name."

At first Julian didn't understand that she agreed to come, but was thrilled with the news when it finally penetrated. "I'll make all of the arrangements," Julian insisted. "All of them. A car will pick you up for the airport. All you do is pack."

"I will bring the sweater I have knitted for Sky and my ideas for your new house, too. Also, we can take a look around for signs of your mother, Julian. I'll show you how to leave her things, your wishes, your thoughts. Now, speaking of the new place you will build, it's nice all those things for your children, but Julian what is the one thing you really want?"

What he really wanted, he thought later, was a small whitewater park so he could practice tricks on waves, like he'd been watching on the YouTube videos of those national sporting events held year round on the great frothing rivers of the United States. He was teaching Sky to play tennis—she was a poor sport like Grey Mars, but unlike Mars, he often let her win. Cloris could build her character with her gentle, but firm hand, Julian loved to make her happy-- no triumphant. With his own private training ground, he could teach her a little about kayaking, or at least play boating on a wave. They both could learn. Kayaking was the last time he had been so supremely, smugly free. He began daydreaming about going back on the river. The pool was outside, he could at least throw in his boat and practice rolling. If it didn't scare her, he could get her the kids' model and see how she took to it.

When the phone rang, he let it go. After it had stopped ringing, and the voice mail began to flash, Julian went and played the message back. Sky's confident voice filled the house, "Juli, We're on our way!" She sang, evidently undeterred even though he had not answered. "We're on our way over after all. We're bringing a lot of stuff. We're going to bake bread!"

The words cut into him, the stars seemed to be oddly aligning. Julian hurried to hastily clean out the refrigerator, and when he heard the garage door begin to slide open, he went to help carry in their packages. And there was his daughter, both blue hands out the window trilling her fingers at him like he was the most important person in her life.

Quite unexpectedly, Grey Mars showed up shortly after Sky and Cloris, shouting "I smell the heaven of fresh baking bread!" Julian thought he might have smelled the bread baking in his office, several miles away, in Westwood, or somehow intuited it. They all stopped to watch him enter, and shed his top layer of clothes. Since it had been raining, it would be something like a quickly performed circus act. First the flourish of the brilliantly printed, over sized umbrella being folded, then the hat came off, taking a spinning flight toward the sofa. The scarf was multiple colors so every lap off his neck revealed another unexpected flash, yellow, green, mustard, red, purple, and then the dreaded blue. Mars shucked off his expensive overcoat—honestly Julian didn't know how he could bear so many clothes it was not cold outside, just damp. Under that was his suit coat, under that, a vest of shimmering Japanese silk, Julian now regretted brining him back so many, after that his tie, once it stopped doing battle with the elegant vest it went limp and then was pulled off like a snake shedding it's skin. Finally Mars rolled up his cuffs, revealing his flashing gold watch the size of a full moon, this he took off and laid tenderly on the dining table like it was a precious love. Once the shirt got unbuttoned, he sighed "ah!" deeply, the bulky strong neck allowed to breath, they seemed to all exhale, too.

"There. Ah! I feel better. Catch, Juli."

As some sort of end mark to his stripping off of the *L.A mover and shaker Grey Mars*, he threw a newspaper at Julian, "I marked the page, but it's all over the Internet, which I know you're patently ignoring these days."

"So what is it now? In brief, please," Julian asked nodding toward Sky who was still within earshot and because Mars, raised in a that kind of household had no filter around the kid, or anyone, really.

"To take the information down to an elevator pitch, there's some sort of pseudo-scientific war, over your dead body, between an agency in Norway and that sperm collection place here in Culver City. You know which one I mean. Where Sky originated from. Both believe they have the rights to your corpse, when the time comes. Not to worry I hired an attorney to get that shit you signed in Culver City retracted. Jeezus, fu—"

"Mars!" Julian yelled, pointing at Sky.

"Sky! You look gorgeous, as always. Cloris, you too! I can't wait to try that bread, I hope you have real butter. Listen,

Juli, so far, I've found thirty-six *blue*, off spring. If there are any other color kids they haven't registered on the website, and got the DNA clearance," he announced with a certain amount of jubilation that always puzzled Julian. Cloris made no comment, but Sky was beginning to jump around, winding up, too. Mars hardly took time to inhale. "That means you are going to get to be a grandfather some day no doubt about it. Women are after you all the time. I get phones calls, emails and letters every day trying to get me to hook you up. And me? Well, fuck, I haven't made a single contribution to the gene pool. I have got to get on this and find love. I need kids, too. It's not like I can do this through sperm donation. How would I ever recognize my own off spring? Red hair? Recessive! Weird green-brown eyes?" He batted a hand on the air, drawing another breath.

Sky turned toward Cloris with her mouth open ready to ask, but already an expert at nipping these kinds of questions before they had a chance to bloom, her grandmother turned her sharply back into the kitchen. This was always the strongest signal to Sky to let the questions drop, immediately, or risk getting sent to her room to read or fold towels.

"Let's get some more bread started," Cloris said firmly, but Julian knew she was going to be pouring herself a finger or two of vodka over crystal ice. Grey Mars always brought out the drinker in Cloris, who cringed at his liberal use of swear words, and choice of topics, but otherwise seemed to genuinely like him, if it did take a bit of hard liquor to wash him down.

"I need love, Juli, just where do I find it? Cloris?"

She fluttered a hand at him, a signal to Mars to zip it so he turned back to Julian, his bright eyes open expectantly, like he all had the answers on the tip of their tongue, but was making him wait.

"I have no wisdom on love, Grey. As you well know, in that I am a total failure," Julian answered quickly to avoid groaning out loud, and he just caught his foot before it could stamp in on the floor. Grey Mars in love was not something Julian ever looked forward to. The stupidity of always choosing the wrong women before the terrible embarrassment (to Julian, he took it personally that his friend was so unreserved with his emotions) over-wooing, then the woman's sensing she had a rich, weak fish on her hook, the long phone calls of his sniveling, begging, the elaborate gifts, and uncalled for grand gestures. Love drained all of Grey's super powers, and Julian could hardly stand to go through it again. The only upside to Mars's terrible accident was that it took him off the market for many long, tranquil months. Julian considered calling in Naomi to slap Mars silly. Or to match-make him with someone suitable, not that he'd ever go with any relationship that didn't provide sufficient misery. Sometimes Julian was convinced Grey Mars was a reincarnated 19th century Russian writer. Or any Russian, really, he had that type of dark mental attitude toward love. *To love is to suffer, to suffer is to love*, well, maybe that was a Woody Allen quote, he thought, but the sentiment was rooted in the Russian soul somehow.

"Maybe you should try a match making service. Like an arranged marriage, Grey," Julian said with an honesty he rarely used with his friend, especially when Sky was around, and it involved affairs of the heart, specifically the elephant sized heart of Grey Mars.

Mars studied him seriously for a few minutes before he let the starving hyena laugh out. It made Julian laugh, too, and then Sky, too, probably because she was relieved some of the tension was being let out of the room.

Grey Mars noticed Cloris's silent appraisal, her slow sipping off the rim of the glass, obviously waiting to be asked what she was thinking.

"What?" Grey asked her.

"I think that may be your very best bet, Grey Mars," Cloris said. And before Sky could ask what his very best bet was, she looked down at her granddaughter and said simply, "We need to find Mr. Mars a proper wife. A real woman who knows the value of give and take, by that I mean someone who can love as full heartedly as he does. Grey never goes half way. And of course, has his same taste in expensive, gaudy jewelry. Also as important, she needs to desperately want children."

Julian turned away to cover his smile, thinking, so Cloris had noticed all the painful nuances of Grey's last fling, too, but had never before commented, on this, or anything. This was a person who could keep her thoughts to herself, something the two of them had in common. Or it could be she just liked to watch the comedy unfold.

"Grey Mars deserves a good woman," Cloris stated.

Julian realized she really did like Mars because typically she would only make a statement if she felt one was required to smooth things over.

"We can do that?" Sky asked. Julian found himself leaning in, too. Mars looked skeptical like not even he believed he could do something as stunningly easy as choosing the right woman.

"Juli?" Mars asked.

"She might have a point, my friend," Julian said, laughing first. This was the first time Mars left the room quietly, taking only his wild umbrella. They all watched.

"Mars! I'm going to take Sky to the American River to learn the kayak basics," Julian called after him. "I ordered her everything today so we can practice rolling in the pool."

"I'm in!" he shouted back, his footsteps following from somewhere in the middle of the house, telling Julian he was about to go to the roof lookout to soul search with his binoculars trained on a certain window down the canyon, under his Frida Kahlo-inspired umbrella. Outside the rare rain tapped lightly on the skylights, a cloud passing overhead darkened the room. Julian and Cloris sighed at the same time.

# Chapter Eleven

Built on the suggestions of Cloris, Grey Mars, Naomi, Rini, and an exorbitantly priced architect, their haven was inside twenty-foot walls. There Julian settled in to tend his children, his investments, read what he felt like, workout, nap and write only when absolutely necessary, in another words when he wanted to look like he was doing something he picked up a pen and doodled in a small notebook. It took three years to get the house and grounds to the point they could move in and spread out comfortably. Julian kept the house in Hollywood, for Grey Mars.

Although she was not the first child he adopted, Sky became a permanent child, by modern standards from the beginning. Julian had formally adopted her when she was just turning eleven, sharing parental rights with the puzzling, free-spirited mother. At that time Sky lived with him eighty percent of the time until she graduated from high school and moved in completely. A year later she showed no signs of leaving, and Julian tried not to pry, push or urge her toward a university, or anywhere. The online courses she was taking seemed to satisfy her, and as long as Cloris approved, Julian was happy to stay out of it. He had no idea what her mother thought on the subject if anything at all. In all these years he had only spoken with her a handful of times. Cloris always had been and always would be the authority on Sky.

Thanks to Grey Mars, Julian had rescued four children from foster care, abandoned for being blue by their mothers to dispassionate strangers. All four were barely out of the toddler stage. All were much younger than Sky, so even with all the court ordered injunctions, the aggressive publicity against the clinic and what not, Julian's sperm was still being sold. Even though Mars finally got his own twin boys, he still took his responsibility as uncle to the blue children as seriously as ever. No more, Julian thought, much more. Most of his blue children loved Mars back, none disliked him, at the very least, he was universally respected by all of the kids, but he loved them all. In this way Mars was superior to Julian, but he had always been full hearted.

Of the four who were abandoned, Royal, and Beryl, were typical boys if no one was around to catch them. They liked to find things to break and climb on, or build, but feared their natural impulses. Both knew punishment. Gentle Sunday Blue who wore flower prints at all times, and Julia, who asked his help to change her name from Blue Melody, during the adoption process, were achingly appreciative of him. Julian, with the help of all of the more responsible adults there, saw to their comfort, their education, gave them allowance, and his clumsy time, trying to patch the wounds that he knew would forever weep. Sometimes he told them about his own mother's disappearance.

"Because you were blue?" Royal asked, at four years old.

"Well, no. I wasn't blue yet," Julian said, but what he filled in was something like the fairytales Sky could spin into silver linings, only a tangled, more embarrassed version. They accepted this, he thought, sadly, as they accepted everything without any resistance or spark of self-will at all.

They usually all started the day collected in the kitchen for breakfast before school so Julian could begin dispensing what he knew about parental love, peeled from the playbooks of Mars, Rini and Cloris. When the food was set down, they set about fixing Julian exactly as he would have done for himself. They knew his habits better than he did. Passing salt, before he asked, handing over a white napkin if someone had set the table with colors (yes, Julian had his peculiarities, too) pushing the cream toward him before he reached for it. That morning they were having eggs, some sort of vegetable stir, and fresh fruit. All his favorites.

"I don't see that Dad has his Tabasco sauce," someone said once the table was reviewed, tiny Julia pushed back her chair to get it.

"Sit down, drink your milk," Julian ordered needing a break from the scrutiny. They dropped their eyes to their glasses and obediently drank up, without missing a beat. No one had ever ordered Julian to drink milk as a child. The food was set before him and the adult left him to do what he wanted with it. He had learned the 'drink your milk' line from Rini and Cloris. The problem was he never really understood how much they should actually take in at each meal.

"When I was a child I ate pickled beets, fish and cheese with coffee for breakfast. I had never heard of Tabasco sauce until I got here to California," he said to soften the blow. They looked up at him round eyed, and if he was not mistaken, a little nervous about how they should respond.

"You don't think that's weird?" Julian asked trying to get them to exhale and let their guarded personalities out, something that only happened when Rini was around.

"Did you ever eat pineapple?" Julia asked smiling a small, demure curve. Like many there, she was a collector, these days it was all things pineapple for reasons she could only explain as, 'it seems like there is some kind of future for me in pineapples.' She was still a sweet child that had not yet hit the tsunami of grief that was thirteen, if she was anything like the others. Julian both hoped and feared she would be.

"I never had a pineapple until I was perhaps twenty. I had seen them in photos and art, but never realized they could be eaten. They looked so rough." They all giggled on cue. Julian did his best not to sigh out loud. None of his stories were new to them, it was like a play they put on each day, breakfast, matinee and evening performance.

If being blue scorched their fragile souls, as it still often did his, they never let on. This is what smashed his heart, his gut, raked at the muscles in his calves, their collective stoicism, their refusal to let anything get them down, even in obvious safety, even when they were entitled to let their pain be known. They kept it locked in. The silent, hidden weeping, those unasked questions, the terrible surrender to accepting whatever might come next was the absolute worst for him. In contrast, Sky had the most fantastic temper tantrums, thirteen being her most volatile year to date although she still had those storms surface often enough to make Julian quite apprehension, even jumpy, when Cloris went home. Sky readily made room for her little bothers and sisters, her confidence in being his full-fledged child made her almost the bully sibling, although she had always been unfailing good as a sibling, mercilessly demanding when it was uncalled for, relentlessly protective, and insistent they fight for their own identities and stop following her around trying to steal her.

"They are only a very few years old, Sky. They were left in uncaring hands believing there would be no rescue. Have patience. We are just more strangers to them." This was Julian's gentle chiding, but Cloris was far more direct. She believed in a good spanking to shape behavior, if need be.

No one was going to have a nervous breakdown under his care without getting support. During these intensely emotional times, Rini was his guiding light. When the children first arrived, she came and stayed for the first six months, cuddling them mercilessly until they gave in to her and would at least sit with their heads resting on hers as she read to them. They played board games, took walks, and sang songs from their favorite musicals. There were things she understood about a wounded human that Julian never wanted to fathom. After Rini's husband died, she moved in permanently to help raise the small children they had been gifted with, as she always said. Julian bought her American citizenship. The place now had four stories, with numerous rooms and four kitchens. Rini lived in a top garrison with her own elevator and kitchenette. Unless invited, Julian never went to her private rooms preferring to leave her free to decorate her perch and rooftop garden as she liked.

The four adopted kids made every effort to fit in, and seemed to love Julian, in their way. In his way, he loved them too. These are my sons, Royal and Beryl, my daughters, Sunday, Julia and Sky, he often found himself practicing this simple introduction for visitors. Truthfully, he had to say Sky's name first or risk the silent treatment and technically, she was not like the others. Sky was unabashed in her affection (and daughterly manipulation) toward Julian, both behaviors he respected as proof of their genuine relationship, something he wished he could get to with these four.

"Good morning Julian," Cloris came into the small dining room and poured a cup of coffee, but didn't sit down. "Good morning my gorgeous Love Bugs. Mmmm I could just eat you up," she said to the children who were stirring their food around with their forks.

"Good morning, Gran," they answered in unison. A subtle drop in their shoulders, a more rounding of their spines told Julian how much they liked Cloris there. He despaired.

"Julian, have you heard from that decorator? I've left several messages and no call back. I have a good mind to have you fire her right now! Those drapes just do not hang as they should, and they don't want to open and close smoothly. Also the color of the new chairs in the Far Den just do not sit right in that room…"

Of all things, she had strong opinions about the interior decoration, so he let her take over as much as she wanted with that, having no interest in it at all. Matching colors or styles seemed a ridiculous thing to worry about. Julian loved all colors, thought they all matched. If he found the furniture uncomfortable he went to stretch out on his own amazing bed that Cloris had chosen for him. Coming from Norway, he never saw the point of heavy drapes and the like. Pillows were for the head, rugs, to keep the floor warmer, the bugs tamped down into the soggy wood, or to wipe your feet on. His childhood home was at least two hundred years old, solid wood almost black in color, small windows, low ceilings, intricately carved inside and out with brightly painted walls, not unlike some of the Amish quilts Rini was so fond of collecting, but still very dark inside.

In the early stages of construction when Cloris asked him to decide on floor coverings, this, it turned out meant, carpet, tile, or wood, he wondered if the cleaners (maid, or whatever was the correct title these days, it confused him what to call the help) should be consulted since they would be dealing with them on the most familiar level. "I'll decide," Cloris answered, concluding that business once and for all.

The only area he cared about was the outside, the one place, he actually had a vision, but often he could see she was holding back with the landscape architect. Cloris did not see the point in palm trees, with their stingy shade, and they were grass, not trees, she had informed him. Palm trees were something Julian would never give up. Succulents were his favorite. Stacks of boulders with plants growing in the cracks caused her to hold her head with both hands and sigh, "too primitive, too primitive."

"Have you seen Sky?" She asked, stroking each child's head as she made her rounds around the table tucking them into their clothes. Lately she wore her hair shorn up one side while on the other side a sheet of angled hair fell to her chin. The new color was a vivid, but not unattractive, orange with matching lipstick. Since her very successful facelift, she had started dressing from the pages of 1970s fashion magazines, a harking back to a time she must have felt very good about herself, Julian thought, trying to picture Cloris at Studio 54 shaking her booty in her ten inch platforms. He wondered if he dared tell her how terrific she looked, but didn't. Women had such strict and confusing rules about these things, silence was always best. Anyway Grey Mars would trumpet it to her when he came by later. Julian could nod in his agreement then.

"Thank you, Gran," each child said in turn. Cloris was busy making her way around the table, mothering them all by manipulating the food on their plates.

"Let me get that for you, Sweetheart. If you are really still thirsty, drink water. You've all had enough milk, I see. I'll remind the cook, again, to only use the small glasses I bought for your serving of mild. So you haven't seen Sky this morning either?"

"Yes, she was just here, lifted a peach from the sideboard, tucked a banana under her arm and went back to work, as she put it. Sky is still all hush-hush with her newest project," Julian said, watching Cloris put a slice of peach on his own plate, waiting as the children were, to see if she was going to cut it up for him, as she had done for them. She was swift with the knife and fork, Julian had to give her that. He let her slice golden quarter moons, without comment.

"That project, such a big secret," Cloris said without elaboration, but Julian knew secrets irked Cloris. She had allowed her only daughter—Sky's mother—secrets and learned her lesson all right.

"You know Grey will keep her in hand," Julian said.

"Yes," Cloris said, as if he was missing the point.

Sky was making an independent movie with Grey Mars, still in the planning stages, all details still under wrap. Julian stayed out of it. Both were rather volatile in the active stages of the creative process. Mars had pronounced Sky a fantastic writer, with a gift for blocking scenes, and maintaining continuity through writing dialogue. Of course she was, he thought, her mother was a successful writer, albeit in that most catastrophic genre called thriller, paranormal romance—gag--- but apparently quite popular. Julian wasn't sure how that kind of story would translate to humanity in general. He hoped not at all.

"Is Rini home?" Julian asked.

"She told me she is going to buy a sewing machine this morning. Julian, maybe these lovely children would just prefer a bowl of Cocoa Locos and a banana with a wedge of lightly buttered toast. They aren't really eating this fare," Cloris said. All four heads snapped to Julian, and their blue faces transformed, not quite into smiles, but something like a glow. Julian got up to get the cereal for them.

"I'm going to the studio. If that designer calls, fire her. I'll do this myself," Cloris said, sounding like she was declaring war on the upholstery gods. Sky got much of her temperament from her grandmother, Julian had learned over the years. Cloris was there most of the time, too, taking up painting, and pottery lessons from Julian's artistic children, and giving lessons herself. Another domain Julian carefully avoided. A dedicated artist of her own brand, Cloris liked to weave, something she brought to them, three looms, each the size of a small car. They needed their own casita, with special cedar lined storage bins for the woolens. Already that weaving clan was working on a *chuppa* for the first Jewish wedding Cloris knew was sure to come *some* day, although she never mentioned Sky's name specifically, not wanting to risk attracting the attention of the evil eye and all. There were other Jewish blue children to pin her hopes on, and she knew them by name, openly courting them to the traditions.

"I'll see you later, Love Bugs," Cloris told them, handed out individual squeezes and left the room.

From somewhere beyond the room, Julian heard Cloris say, "Sky, what are you wearing?"

"Fashion is about the unexpected," Sky responded, like she had the line prepared for weeks.

"No. You get those *nonnie-pies* covered up. Go change now," Cloris commanded. Their footsteps matched as they walked together back to Sky's room. Julian felt all was going to be right with the world that day.

The four at the table finished their cereal and asked permission to leave. Julian granted it. After that they went through their ritual of lining up and thanking him with a brief hug.

"Have fun today. I mean really have fun. It's summer vacation," Julian told them.

"Rini is going to teach me to sew today," Sunday announced unexpectedly.

"Then you are certain to learn." Julian responded. Following her lead the other three filled him in on their plans to which Julian promised to check in with them at lunch at the pool when they had their swimming lesson. Their confiding their plans to him felt like some sort of small break through, but he was afraid to prolong it. After all these years, he felt like giving them gold stars.

"Go out and have fun," Julian ordered in a tone he hoped sounded sincerely tender.

After that, he watched them troop out hoping that once they were out of his sight they would break free and become in some way jubilant just to be kids. Bounce around a little. Down the hall he heard Sky being ordered back in for another change of clothes. Her sigh could have blown off the roof. Julian smiled.

Sky, was so easy for him to love. It felt like she was made of his blood, his bones. And if she would stop nagging him about trying to find "real, romantic" love in the form of a wife, he would consider her perfect. No matter what the rest of the world's standards may be he was supremely proud of her. Sky excelled in kayaking, and any other sports she decided to tackle.

Sky's confidence in being Julian's true child made her almost the bully sibling, although she had always been unfailing good as the big sister, protective, loving and merciless in her insistence that they always follow her commands the first time they were given. Anyway, she never complained about them, even forgave their most grievous sins, like keeping Julian's attention even after she had noisily entered the room, or for getting better grades, and woe to sweet Julia who could sing with an operatic power and quality, the one thing Sky coveted over any talent, but was not born with. Julia persisted with her music lessons four days a week no matter what subtle pressures Sky tried to exert, so perhaps there was progress there, too.

During the school year when there were fewer siblings around, the five of them spent much time together making home movies, and writing comedy bits that Julian refused to indulge, if it was bad, he told them to start over, giving his expert opinion and tips. If they refused to work to improve he refused to watch.

Guiding them like this was his greatest responsibility, he felt. While sometimes he secretly felt he was being too harsh, it wasn't like he was chewing down whole lemons, snapping apples in half with his bare hands, or shooting at them with live ammunition when they were ill. Truth was, he was grateful for them, and he never wanted them to leave. Many came to stay for weeks over the summer, a time Julian looked forward to every year.

From the time of that discovery of the four orphans on, Julian actively searched for any blue child in trouble, and kept his door open should any others land in that foster care system. To his knowledge, besides speeding and parking tickets, none of his blue children had committed a crime, done anything violent, or ended up in anyway incarcerated. They were children, and that was all. He wished the world would be kinder to them just for that alone.

Julian gladly paid for university tuition, but if a blue offspring had a business idea, he left it to Naomi or Mars to review the plan and either shatter their dreams or get them started. Few passed the funding tests, but they were all still very young, as Naomi was fond of saying to them, offering the box of tissue to mop those adolescent tears, but never budging on her decision. The first and last court was Naomi.

All blue children were free to show up at his door with a DNA test as admission requirement. If they were minors they needed a parent. They all still wanted answers, as if he had them, which of course he didn't. Still, he welcomed them. Over time, there were several he put through a private school for blue children some wise person founded and brought to his attention. It was a fine school that had quickly become integrated. Occasionally he bought cars, clothes, tutors, and often provided rather intense psychotherapy that did nothing to alleviate the sorrows of a sad child.

Sadly, Julian had no words of condolence for any of them. After all the years of being blue, waking up from any type of dream was still the hardest moment, when that first flash of his blue hand reaching for a sip of water reminded him. After that few moments passed he quickly moved into back into acceptance. It helped that his own sorrow was greatly blunted in exchange for all that he had gained by turning blue: Sky, his extended family, all of his children, really, even the remote, antagonistic, accusatory or annoying ones drew some measure of pride from him. His own vanity over being ashamed of being blue, well, that was his personal immaturity.

Now it was summertime and dozens of his blue children were enjoying the delights of his lake-sized pool, the kayak playground, and all the other amenities. One of his newly arrived daughters, a famous one, sat across from him wiping a flowery scented cream into the periwinkle skin of her strong forearm. The tumble of long shimmering hair was dyed an intense purple, complimenting and intensifying what most were trying to hide, her blue skin. The turn of her head, the perfect symmetry of her face, the cheekbones, and perfect chin reminded him very much of his lost mother. Julian felt unusually tense and on guard with her, this spoiled and therefore often abrasive young woman.

"You have no idea how we suffer. We're made fun of."

"What?!" He mocked.

She flipped her hair, offering her perfect profile. This one didn't need his money. A highly paid fashion model of incredible fame she could afford her own cars, jewelry and therapy. This one was also slow to get to her point.

"I feel tortured, and you sit there so, so, so silently! How can you?"

Julian sighed, checked his watch, and then scanned the horizons. Sky was due to rescue him for a game of doubles tennis.

"There are advantages if you choose to use them." This was a patent line of his, sometimes it soothed, usually in offspring like this one, it promoted tantrums; he just couldn't break the habit of saying it. Life *was* what you made of it, if you could afford it, and she certainly could.

The corners of her eyes turned down, that famous mouth drew into a pucker before it spat out, "They want to experiment on us. They want our blood. Literally."

The badly abused word *literally* always made him bluster. His shrug was to indicate both boredom with the topic and his shaky acceptance of being its victim, too. After all, it wasn't like he wanted this either. Back in the day his life had been one of standing out, the rather famous bad boy on his way to superior stardom, comfortable in his own pale, Norwegian skin and golden hair. The pain that shot into his heart was always swift and brief. The past was over he reminded himself. *Look at your own hand.*

A noisy game of volleyball was started in the pool. Of his children there that day, no two had exactly the same color skin. They were all terrific swimmers, and smart, rather gentle as a people, he thought again feeling a twinge of satisfaction. Even this gorgeous specimen had no real edge to her complaints, it was almost like she had been rehearsing them, or someone fed her the lines.

"You must know where this comes from!" She wept dramatically.

Why did so many still think he could reverse this, but intentionally did not?

"I have no idea how to change your color," he said searching the rolling greens that lead to the path Sky usually followed to rescue him from the pool side interviews.

Julian thought she made an outstanding living from her unique and beautiful face, body and yes, 'delicious skin color', as magazines were so fond of describing it. In short, he found her protests disingenuous. A bird flew across the water and landed on a floating chair. Julian drummed his fingers on the tabletop impatient to get to the game of tennis with his some of his more congenial off spring.

"You are blue, adjust," Julian said, picking up his pen to pretend to write.

Twisting the pen from his fingers with an unexpected strength she threw it at the bird, which fluttered away in plenty of time. Her eyes glistened. "I don't ever want to change my color! Why can't you just tell them where you got it? If more go there to be blue they'll leave us alone. We'll blend in. We'll have blue partners we can marry. *We can't marry a sibling!* Life will be simple then. And perfect." Self-satisfied, she crossed her arms over her chest and sat back.

"Ahhhh, the naïveté of youth. Life will never be perfect," he said bluntly, but didn't admit that marriage was something he would never understand. Julian had never been in love, except as a parent, or friend. Romantic love had proven to be so elusive he never thought of it any more. Occasionally he met up with Talia for a couple of days of something that was like a state of loving-

112

lust. Otherwise wouldn't he ask her to come home with him, wouldn't she ask to go? After a day or two they both ran out of ways to thrill each other and he returned alone, glad of the release. This concept of true love, he was convinced, had to be something manufactured for story value alone, a way to create tension as no other story line could. Even the threat of death was not as strong an arc as the potential for destroying this vital function of the heart.

"How did it happen to you?" This time she whispered, a new tact. Julian shrugged.

As if he were hiding it, this insidious plot of deliberately turning blue. As if he never wanted to feel normal again. And then Julian thought of rolling his kayak in those exotic waters. Eating salted watermelon, with gnarled, absurd or even weird plants he'd never seen before, wolfing down exotic tacos in blue shells. Bulge eyed fish with invisible skin. Roasted insects. Scalding liquor. Peyote. Others had eaten all of it, too, drank more, and got just as high, and all remained un-blue. This reminded Julian of his plans to meet with the Lights, Camera, Action crew on the river, very soon with Sky. An annual event they all looked forward to, especially with the advent of the new helmet-mounted cameras for the hilarious post mortems at dinner. Soon he would try to initiate his other four, although he was certain Sunday should not be pressured. Even the calm, clear pool water scared her to near panic, the only time he had seen true, unbridled emotion and tears from her. Swimming lessons were tense and another way to make Julian feel he was over-parenting, but Rini insisted she would become more confident each time she went in and came out safely.

"Julian! Why aren't you listening to me?" She blinked her own shimmering eyes back at his, trying to use their power on him. After Hollywood actresses, scandalized reporters, woman trying to seduce him disguised in all manner of professions, and of course, Sky, he was immune to piercing eyes, but didn't let on.

"Why can't you just enjoy this splendid day with your brothers and sisters?" *And me,* he wanted to add.

With one smooth sweep of her body, she turned away from the table to dig into her enormous, expensive bag full of lady things. Taking up a point of toast, he began meditating on its perfect crunch when a flash of a blue crossed his periphery. Her foot was on the table, she was painting her toenails the same intense sparkling purple as her hair. The navicular size of her shapely, but enormous foot shocked him. Could this human really be a product of his own body?

"Take your foot off the table! We're eating!" He snapped. She dabbed the tiny paintbrush at the air, blinking at him slowly with her gorgeous countenance. He almost suggested she go into acting, but he was certain she had been given that suggestion many times before. She put her foot back on the ground.

"Do you know how exhausting it is for me to be Li-Si Blue?"

Her full name was Lilac Silk Blue. Invariably his half-white children all had *blue* stuck into their names somewhere. Some bore the expected Teal, Turquoise, Ultramarine, Violet, Indigo, Lilac, Beryl, Royal, Azure, Cerulean, Cobalt, and Indigo. Others were given the more creative variations: Mirror Blue Lake, Sweet Blue, Stormy Blue Water, Ella Blue, July Sky Blue, Blue Iris, Eva Lilac, Blue Rain, Azul, Ut Te Blue, Loyalty Bleu, Icy Blue, Blue Ice, Sparkle Blue, Celestial Blue, Blue Angel, Sapphire Glow, Misty Blue Dawn, Summer Blues Nightfall, Maribleu-- lovely girl in spite of that dreadful name-- oh he could name an entire wall of blue paint chip colors assigned to his hapless children. They deserved real names, at the very least he thought, picturing blue toddlers innocently sucking their tiny fingers purple.

Those with black mothers were the most well-adjusted of his children. Their eyes were a sparkling brown, green, deep blue, even black and their skin colors were usually a deep, rich plump grape color, or a burnt purple, or a more unique dusted plum color, glorious in its depth. The exception was his most robust, dare he say, interesting son, a strongly muscled Michelangelo-sculpture of a young man (obviously his mother had her own fantastic genetic sequence to contribute to the breeding of her one child). She named her son-- their son-- Tauro. Unlike his other children Tauro- who liked to call himself, Fine China Blue, fully embraced his midnight blueness, which only seemed to deepen in the bright sunshine of Southern California. Unlike his other children, Tauro was a fighter. Julian would have liked to call him El Toro, the bull, and had to threaten to take away his gym privileges to keep him from brawling in the rowdy local bars, or maybe they were calm tourist bars until he showed up. Tauro was one who liked to face the approach. And prevail, as it were. He protected Julian, seemed to really love him. Julian adored him even when his son boisterously hoisted him over his head before launching him into the pool fully clothed. Even Sky accepted him, and if Julian was not mistake, she held a certain admiration toward him, too. They had spent hours together playing chess under the shade of the palms. Julian wished with all his heart Tauro would show up just then and save him from Li-Si.

Outside of Tauro's self-invented name, Fine Blue, his half black children bore the usual names they would have got anyway: Kenya, Jamal, Tovante, L'Shay, November, Paris, Alexis, Langston, Jonah, Maylon, Gilispie, Maya Angelou, Ray Dawn-Dawn, Bernard, and the like. Now that many of his black children were turning eighteen, on the whole they seemed to stop by just to pay a courtesy call, but then often stayed for long stretches of time because, he believed, they liked it there. They liked him, and they enjoyed getting to know their siblings. He always got the sense they were trying to reassure him that they were all right, in the opposite way his half-white children were trying to wring his guilt. They were all curious why he sold his sperm, or so much of it. And frankly, he always told them truthfully, he sold his sperm because as a blue, cast off-has-been with newly minted super genes, and a mountain of medical bills, he needed the God damned money. The story of his father shooting him was kept locked in the tight inner circle, never mentioned, not even to Sky, but the near-death of Grey Mars was widely known. They understood his agony at that point in time, young as they were, they understood loyalty and brotherly love in the face of adversity.

"You are each a miracle. I have a tribe," he told them and meant it.

As with all the skin colors in the world, his blue children also suffered the prejudice of hues within their tribe. The most unfortunate ones, he thought, were those who tended toward the gray shades, it made them look dusty and sickly, like his boy Soulful Blue whose sense of outcast rendered him a reclusive, pensive adolescent, but among them all he was the only one who wanted to sit for hours to secure the compound. Julian adored it when Soul came to sit and talk to him. The boy was chock-a-block full of incredible ideas. Nothing deterred him from the tedious task of engineering the required number sequences, or whatever it was he did, so the gates, and outside doors could not be opened without permission. His personal mission was to keep the public out of the elaborately guarded premises. The boy's superior genius and melancholy were probably to be expected; his mother was some sort of computer whiz, too. Social isolationists, those, Mars had declared them. She was also one of the mothers who daily exhorted Julian to put their child back into the real world so he would learn to be proud of who he was although she never left her own house, did nothing to stand out in any way that showed evidence of risking social punishment for earning pride of self for her differences. Julian was told she liked to wear self-designed, new age clothes, inside the safety of her house. Julian let Soulful live there as he pleased with his pets, mainly well trained dogs. For Julian, Soulful was another stand out son seeking refuge from a freakishly stupid world. Julian knew just how he felt.

Soulful's mother wasn't the only mother to protest his allowing them to collect and hibernate in his compound as they called it. Easy for someone who came with a regular, accepted color, those being in the flesh tones of full moon white to deep ironstone black, learning 'pride of blue' was easy to insist upon. Try being blue, he thought: for one damn day, airbrush on the make up and go out into the public you fecund bitches! Oh, those mothers had it easy with only one, maybe two blue children to answer to. He, Julian, now had dozens weighing on his conscience. That they chose him for safe harbor, and that he could provide it gave him immeasurable satisfaction.

"Listen to me. Why will you never tell anyone?" she cried, jiggling Julian's attention back to her by shaking the table.

"It was most likely some genetic tripwire," he started to tell Li-Si, as he noticed with alarm one of his boys wrestling a piece of hard fruit against a very sharp, folding knife. He half leapt out of his chair, hollering. "Jaden Blue! Put that knife down before you slice your own dick off." Jaden Blue peered back, his gaze a frozen, and embarrassed stare, before looking down at the knife and piece of fruit in his hand like he couldn't remember how they got to be there. Well, Julian would have never promised a high level of intelligence to anyone who bought his sperm, in either carnation, white or blue. He always thought of himself as book smart, he could learn things, but figuring out complicated puzzles? He was not on the high level of Grey Mars, Rini or Naomi.

"Don't move Jaden Blue," Julian commanded, but gently, as he stood. One of the wait staff was already there. To keep the place from being destroyed he had learned to employ competent keepers, much like they did in any well-run zoo, he mused, thinking maybe it was a compound after all. This made him uncomfortable.

"Well Julian?" Li-Si breathed as if hers was the life in peril. "Did it ever once occur to you that you would be bringing all of us into this?" She waved her hand at paradise, in his opinion.

"Not even once."

Julian watched as the fruit was expertly sliced, and the knife was taken away with the peels before he said to his daughter, "I didn't think into the future at all. As I have told you all, I was stoned, and actually *blue* in every sense of the word, so I was just trying to find something to do so I did not go insane. I was made to feel that I was making some sort of contribution to science."

"And by the way, Li-Si, if you haven't noticed, this is not such a bad place to hide from the world."

"Yeah, hide. I don't want to have to hide," she said. Her slender hand flicked back her hair dramatically.

"Well, I do." Julian rejoined. The garden was a park with fountains, flowers and contemplation zones. His whitewater play park was featured in a magazine. There was an actual forest to explore with zip lines, there was a workout park, and he'd built art studios for those so inclined. Of course every room had a computer, a television, a shower. The library was immense. Didn't all this say love, or at the very least: I take responsibility?

"I want to know what happened!" Li-Si cried.

Some scientists thought it was from a virus, an insect bite, or in the water, or strange native food. Julian thought it depended on which comic book hero they preferred. From his Aqua Man days, and his love of rivers he preferred the water theories. There is a lot of water in the world, and before the Mexico rivers Julian had traveled the blue marble surfing, whitewater kayaking, rafting and yes even canoeing on calmly undulating rivers heading south for one hundred miles. And yet, he was secretly certain he did know where it had occurred. The week before Mexico there had been a place in the Amazon where they had been forced to hole up when a small army of tiny brown savages chased them off their route through the jungle. The men wielded the spears, the women the big, sharp knives. Male or female, didn't seem to matter those tiny naked beings could all haul ass, as he recalled, their hot breaths on their necks, primitive need for blood letting flashing in their blades. In their panic, the group had stumbled upon a secluded grotto with a tantalizing waterfall only he was brave enough to go off lying down, feet first on a thin, inflatable camping mattress. He could not get enough of that waterfall, that pool of luscious pinkish water. He washed in it and secretly brewed his own coffee with it, too. During the week of waiting to make their escape (they all had satellite phones, credit cards with no limit, and even guns; they had never been in any real danger, but a helicopter seemed like a wimp out and who wants to murder another human on a vacation?) he had noticed the blue color seeping into the sharp edges of his scapha on both of his ears, and his lower lip, even as he denied it to himself. And then he'd thought it had disappeared. From that time on though, when the entire crew of strong men were daily more beaten down, he felt he had hit some sort of pinnacle of fantastic health, certain to tip off at any time and crash. Besides the mental torture of turning blue, physically, that time still had not arrived.

"Come on, Dad," Sky ordered. "You've suffered enough. Miss Li-Si, I believe you ordered a massage?" Sky waved toward the handsome masseuse that stood at one of the borders to the pool area, bowing slightly. Li-Si clapped her hands, grabbed her bag and swept off in a sulky breeze.

"I ordered it for her," she told Julian. "Just say the word and we'll counsel her out of this visit by tomorrow afternoon."

Julian chuckled. "She said something I've never heard before."

"What would that be?" Sky had lately taken to reassuring Julian with all the pats and back rubs Cloris had spent years applying to both of them in times of stress. Now that she was as tall as she was and her eyes had settled into a deep blue, her hair flanking her waist, Julian had to remind himself, frequently, that he didn't have to take orders from her.

"She said she wanted to discover the source she believes turned me blue because she wanted others to drink the water

118

forming new blue tribes to date and marry. Just who would deliberately take that treatment?"

Sky stopped to look in the direction of Li-Si, whose shimmering silk wrap fluttered on the breeze as she dramatically wrapped it around her looking gorgeous.

"Do you think she pays for her own personal sunbeam to follow her around like that?" Julian asked Sky, but she did not seem to hear him.

"Well, there is more to her than I thought. Wanting to marry into a blue tribe. Hmmm. Did you notice if she had pierced ears? I still can't decide about those." Sky finally said. She turned to him, "no tattoos, I promise." They walked shoulder to shoulder for a few more steps, he was admiring the newly planted trees, the smell of jasmine had faded, so it was truly summer, spring burned out with the subtle extinguishing of that delicate, favorite scent. Sky stopped again. Julian could feel the build up of whatever she was going to say, and only hoped it was not that she decided to flit off to some university somewhere. He just wasn't ready.

She carefully raked her hair off her forehead using her fingers. "So, Dad, I've decided that I'd like to make a documentary about you, and us, the blues. I've already started with all the footage of that first kayaking trip with Grey and the Lights, Camera, Action crew."

A documentary about him was not a new idea. After every vaguely worded interview he had given, the subject always came up. Julian had also secretly watched the footage they had shot on that trip thousands of times looking for clues, but he found none and said nothing.

"Sky, well," he tried to make his mouth form in the shape, of a "no," but gave up when he realized he must look like a fish kissing the surface of the water. "Oh, all right," he said. Julian could tell everyone no, but Sky. Usually Cloris, Naomi, even Rini, could be counted on to be around to say it for him, but Sky had picked her moment well. Not only was Julian without the sensible women flanking him, but he was already so emotionally flattened by the experience of Li-Si's interview, and subsequent scold he was just grateful to have Sky holding his hand just then.

"I know it's manipulative, and I'm sorry" Sky said, "but it's a good story. Important. There are a few things I think the world should know about us. Also, it's a place for me to start. I feel like I can't move on without getting this out. I want to be a filmmaker, like you."

"There is nothing worse than trying to keep down a story you need to tell," Julian said knowing the truth of this so well. Sky was looking up at him, squinting one eye against the sun. He wanted to hug her, but by hug he meant keep her safe from the ridiculous vagaries of the world forever. Hugs were so fleeting, just the briefest suggestion of protection, he thought. No wonder some people objected to them.

"I have some conditions for approval," Julian said. "Beryl, Royal, Sunday and Julia are all off limits. You can mention that some children have been abandoned, but that is all. I will not give you my permission, as their parent, to tell a story that belongs to them."

"Okay. I understand," Sky said.

"Say you promise."

"I absolutely promise. And we will negotiate all stories that are yours."

"You'll be a fine filmmaker Sky Dot," Julian said, meaning it.

She squinted up at him, also holding back her usual spontaneous hug, he could see her hands clench with the effort, but they were both careful not to reveal too much to the others.

"You have light eyes," Julian said. "You should wear your sunglasses."

"You think I'll get cancer?"

"I think you might miss important details with one eye closed like that and the other wheeling toward your nose," Julian teased.

"So is this about improving my game?"

"It's always about improving your game Blue Dot."

# Chapter Twelve

Julian and Mars had considered many places to build the estate. They both agreed San Francisco would be probably be the most accepting, but Julian could not feel at home there. The rapid paced place was too wet, too foggy, too familiar in a deeply buried, disturbingly Nordish way. The ocean was freezing and rough. The traffic baffled him. Also, most of his offspring lived in the Los Angeles area, the place Julian considered home. The only location that felt right was a few miles from Julian's Hollywood Hills home, there in Beverly Hills. Locating ten acres with a disintegrating mansion was easier than he imagined. The old house could not be saved, so it was unceremoniously cleared away. After that, building the place became something like the trial of Sisyphus, but with the help of a small army, they finally prevailed.

No one just knocked on Julian's door to be elegantly received. There was a gate with a guard and cameras to record events. Soulful was in the midst of making the funnier takes into a short film he planned to show some night on an outdoor screen he was rigging up. He thought the birthday celebration for Grey Mars might be comical enough. Julian saw bits and pieces and approved. They were sitting together in the solarium that Soulful had set up his computers, workstation, and pets. Julian did much of his resource management, investing and the like online, and this meant Soulful had to make sure it was kept secure. An odd message had come up that morning, he went to report it to Soulful who spent their first twenty minutes together changing passwords and looking over the encrypted history behind the English words, a language he seemed to read with the ease of English.

"It's secure," Soulful said, satisfied.

"I was wondering if we could plan to do something together. I mean outside of here. Don't you ever get restless being here?" Julian said after Soulful gave him a long knotted explanation of what he was working on.

"Ever think about caving?" Soulful asked Julian, seemingly out of the blue, an expression he tried to avoid even in his own thoughts, but there it was anyway.

"Caving? As in exploring caves? As a child I used to spend a lot of time exploring caves, ice caves, stone caves. They do weird things to my mind," Julian said simply. There was a wine cellar in the house that Julian would never go in there either, but he said nothing. It wasn't a fear, more like a caution.

"Claustrophobia?"

Julian shook his head, as he gently pushed a mottled color cat off his leg. The dogs kept a respectful distance, watching him with beseeching eyes. From experience he knew that if he pet one, they would all come wagging and panting and shoving their wet noses into his palm until Soulful ordered them off. Then they would slink away to watch him with even more wounded expressions. Julian who understood rejection, looked away.

"Something from the Greek myths?" Soulful asked. Julian shook his head. "I have to go visit my mother today." There was absolutely no upbeat in his flat tone.

"Do you want me to go with you?" Julian asked him gently.

"Naw. She's harmless. But listen, I'm going to have to get someone to help cover this security."

Thanks to Soulful, the path to entering their home was rigorous, and for good reason. The world was full of people who wanted something from Julian, even marriage, but especially money. If you were a blue person claiming a relationship to Julian, a DNA test was required just to get a pass to park. The police, mayor or UPS delivery people were all treated the same. Only Grey Mars, Cloris, Rini and Naomi could come and go freely, through a separate, rather secret driveway.

"I think we'll be okay. Unless you already have someone in mind," Julian said.

"I'll be back tonight. We need to talk about the increase in drones that are going overhead and some other air-over-surveillance."

"I don't understand," Julian said. *To think*, he thought, *he was going to ask Soulful how he could arrange to meet a sincere woman*. Julian was experiencing some kind of ache whenever he talked with Talia lately. She suggested he was ready to find a woman. Well, that plan was immediately dropped.

"I know. We'll go over it in detail. Make a plan. See what all is needed," Soulful said.

"We already have nets to keep the seagulls out of the fish habitats," Julian said lamely.

"I know. But what I'm talking about is we seem to be under surveillance. And I'm not sure what we can do about that without real experts coming in."

"Are we in peril?" Julian asked.

"Mild peril, maybe," Soulful said.

"Mild peril? I don't believe such a thing can exist. By definition peril is danger, and danger is, well dangerous."

"Just don't worry. I'll be back in a few short hours and we can go over everything in detail. Nothing is about to happen," Soulful said.

Nevertheless, early that evening, some type of agents from the American government came to the guard tower flashing badges and asking for the representative of the commune, as the guard relayed.

"If they don't have some kind of warrant to enter, keep them outside. I'll be right there,"

Julian immediately called Grey Mars, Naomi, and his attorney. Julian texted Soulful who responded almost instantly: *I'm almost home*. The kid must have the fastest thumbs on earth, Julian mused, and then as an after thought he hoped he wasn't driving and texting.

Once Julian arrived, they bristled, as always, shocked by his blueness and no one offered to shake his hand. Julian didn't offer his either. He had learned that once someone had hold of your hand, well, they had a hold of him.

"We are investigating a problem with a satellite. Interference seems to be coming from here," one said bluntly, accusing him.

"What does a satellite have to do with us? How would a satellite get bothered from here?" Julian asked another dozen questions, another tactic he had learned from reading about practices of successful negotiators. By instinct, he knew they were guilty, but he hadn't the foggiest notion of how or why or which off-spring, and Soulful was not yet home to route out the mischief maker.

"Your computers," the serious woman answered, raising her eyebrows like he was actually playing dumb.

He wasn't technologically savvy and he didn't want to be, but he was smart enough to be worried. "Did you write down my attorney's number?" he asked her.

"Sir we are not going to drop this."

"Do you expect me to think that you will?"

After they left he called his computer geniuses together into the largest room in the house.

"Just who the fuck is fucking with a government satellite?" In times of stress Julian parented like his father, sometimes he just could not suppress that aggressive man. If only he could snap an apple in half, he would do it just then.

The girls laughed rather jubilantly, as if they'd won some sort of contest, right after that they all immediately went silent.

Before Julian could sort it out, it was relayed to him that another important visitor was sitting in the south den. "You'd better go now," his secretary said, giving him the nod. Julian hurried there. This young man was white, but Julian didn't need a DNA test to know he was also his first and only white child, Lana's boy. The day just kept getting harder, he thought massaging his own temples.

"I need a few more minutes if you will just wait for me here. This is not a rejection. I have something to finish just this minute that I have to see to first." Julian told him. "And for your own sake, you haven't told anyone who you are?"

"I haven't told anyone who you are," he countered, lifting that famous Julian-of-old brow. "I did date one of your daughters to do a secret DNA test though. To be sure."

Julian threw his hands in the air at the absurdity of such chicanery. "Make yourself at home. Call on that phone there and order anything you'd like to eat or drink. I shall return as soon as I can. If you can't wait, make an appointment with my secretary and we'll try again."

"My name is Harmony Lane," he called. This stopped Julian.

"Your mother named you Harmony?" But Julian thought, no wonder it's so hard to take women seriously."

"She's an actress. It's what they do. I call myself Lane."

"Lane it is," Julian said hurrying out.

"Julian, before you go, I wanted to tell you, I'm an attorney, politically active, and I've been keeping my eye on you."

"Meaning?"

"I think you're going to need my help."

"I appreciate that you came in peace," Julian said without really wanting to.

Julian went back to the meeting, wondering what kind of sibling rivalry Lane's presence was going to stir up among his blue children.

Once in the room Julian opened with, "What have you to say for yourselves?"

"They should know," one said flippantly, even crossing her arms for some sort of asinine punctuation.

"Know what?" Julian asked pointing both fingers at her.

"That we might be blue, but we have the right not to be monitored by them like were some aggravating terrorists."

"They should know we are capable of defending ourselves," another said.

"That is the last thing *they* should know!" Julian cried. "Has it occurred to you that Americans love a good search and destroy mission? Consider history you genius idiots, I beg you."

The image of fierce Tauro after a fight came instantly to him, his gut wrenched. Julian could see where this all might be headed. He hoped the outside world had not also been making these same connections ahead of him.

"I think you may need a white lobbyist," Lane's strong voice came from the door.

The energy in the room paused and changed direction creating some sort of emotional cyclone waiting to be unleashed. Julian almost ran for cover. Everyone rattled something until someone finally said, "How did you get to be white?"

Julian wondered how such intelligent, perceptive humans could also be so Goddamn dense in the very same moment.

"This is Lane. Seems he was god sent just now to help us avoid war with our own country."

"What war?" Lane cried, but he didn't back out of the room. Julian's chin lifted. Before another word could be said, his geniuses started up again.

"We could hire Dutch engineers, build our own island."

"And become just the absolute, perfect target?"

"Why not just stop screwing with satellites?"

"They are watching us. All we are doing is recreating," one of his daughters said. "We have taken out dozens of drones a week."

"What are drones?" Julian shouted into the room. It brought silence.

"Those small buzzing airplanes the paparazzi and government fly over the place. We've been knocking them out and crushing them."

All this time Julian thought those were the model planes the kids were building and flying in some sort of new wave sporting event. Those could take photos?

The argument raged for a few more minutes until Lane waved his hands in the air. Silence did not find the room for some minutes.

"Tampering with a satellite will cause your arrest," Lane said. "Can you imagine how time in prison would go for a Blue? Even a day? It's not like any of you can run and hide anywhere either, even with Julian's vast wealth."

This silenced the last rumblings. The words terrified Julian. He could imagine the nightmare of prison for a Blue. Even on recent outings to amusement parks, people had still been quite unkind.

"If you need an enterprise, why don't all you geniuses get busy inventing some useful things like a comfortable bicycle seat or high heels women can actually run in?" Lane asked.

Julian turned to study Lane. He was old enough to be that child Lana had claimed so long ago to be carrying. Maybe it was this connection to someone he knew to be conniving that he was a bit suspicious. Maybe it was his color, Julian's first color, or the way he stood there looking around the room, superior. There was something irritating about the way he had followed Julian through the house, to that room when he asked him to wait. The inner voice that Julian had always relied on told him not to trust this. There was a special button on Julian's cell phone that he pressed. Within minutes the security guard arrived.

Julian took Lane by the elbowing, walking him to the door, and asked him to make an appointment to speak with him later.

And then he asked the security guard to give him the information he needed to make an appointment with him and then to escort him to his car. They left immediately.

The room began to buzz with chatter, switching Julian's attention. He dropped into the chair, exhausted and yes, rather frantically worried. They were going to need a specialized attorney for sure, but he was certain he could get them out of this satellite debacle. Lane was wrong about that one thing. Money changed the way the law dealt with you. That was the real truth of the justice systems all over the world, even in America. The buzz in the room grew steadily, but now he could hear the real arguments in the under current. Julian had seriously misjudged his offspring. All along they had been silently enraged, plotting against humanity even.

*For there was never yet philosopher*
*that could endure the toothache patiently.*

The line came to him without wringing it from his memory, a striking moment of clarity: the future through his rebel children's eyes. This was not the mark he intended to leave, but Julian thought sadly, he was not going to live forever to parent them to right. No he was not.

"All of you, listen to me. I am not going to allow anyone to stay here if they are going to cause problems for this house. I don't know what those of you involved have been thinking, but this is a home with small children. *My children* that I have promised to keep safe, and I am going to do that at all costs. I don't care to have the United States government barging into my home and turning it upside down. Or give them any cause for suspicion to increase their surveillance of us. So if you can't follow the house rules, you need to pack up and leave. Now. Until further notice the internet is tightly monitored." Julian commanded.

There was some rumbling, but no one left the room.

Julian went and stood in the center of them dramatically like he had something to announce when really he was trying to quickly organize some sort of quick stop-gap plan.

"I think we are all getting a little stir crazy here. So what I have been thinking about for the last few weeks is for those of you who are willing I think it's time we all went on an adventure. Grey

Mars, Sky, and the original crew that went down to South American with us on that first trip always take an annual kayaking refresher on the American River. We have been thinking about retracing our steps on that trip maybe next year. But, everyone that wants to go needs to learn to kayak well enough. Of course we can use raft support, too, but if you are interested in boating, you have to learn. We can get excellent instruction on the South Fork of the American river. It's camping, of course. And I'll hire the experts up there to teach you how to paddle. While we are there, I do promise to tell you everything I remember. Again, if you plan to kayak, there will be training involved. And it isn't for everyone. We'll start rolling lessons in the pool tomorrow morning at ten. If you are leaving, please check out with security so we can let your families know that you have left."

All sound left the room, just for a moment before it again erupted, and Julian was certain from the general buzz that he was on to something. These were creative, restless adolescents who needed more to occupy their time. The place was too confining. Julian sighed. For most of them school started in September, he only needed to keep this all under wraps for a few more weeks. And have Soulful put the security team on a more watchful eye on the computer doings.

"You're going to need to sign up or something. We need a way to keep track of everything. There's a lot to organize so we need volunteers to each take a share," Julian added. There was the unmistakable rumbling of Grey Mars coming toward the room, with others. Their movement was swift and purposeful, so they were bringing information. Sighing slowly as he ran his fingers through his hair, Julian hoped he did not just step into the biggest pile of parenting shit ever plopped down by a near-father.

"Can I bring my girl friend?" Someone asked.

"No girl friends, no boy friends. Experienced kayaking friends or relatives, yes. Your parents are also going to be invited. I know they all can't come, but we're going to need a crew of adults to help keep the lid on," Julian said. That divided the room, but he was adamant. Even with the help of his close friends, they were vastly outnumbered by all of these bored, overly bright adolescents who were apparently, craving a rebellion.

# Chapter Thirteen

At poolside, a few mornings later, Julian stood on one side of the pool, with Grey Mars, looking stronger, happier and healthier than he had in ages. Of course Julian suspected Botox and perhaps he had his lower lids de-puffed, but he would never bring it up. Anyway, he would just prefer to assume it was a powering down of Grey's over-active, restless being, and that this reinvigoration was due to an inner personal happiness and not the first flush of another ill-fated love affair. Having his two young boys had calmed him down. Maybe they were both just aging, in their forties now, although Julian did not look any different from the day he bloomed blue. There weren't any gray hairs, sagging muscle tone, or even any fine lines. It didn't rhyme nicely, but maybe blue didn't crackle either. Not that it mattered. He'd prefer his own natural color to this, and he pitied all the blue off-spring he had accidentally put into the world for having to suffer it, too.

Grey Mars was bouncing on the balls of his feet, clapping his hands and rolling his shoulders in great stretches getting ready for coaching work. Of course he was wearing his Water Logs, a long sleeved shirt, a hat, a whistle around his neck, and held a long orange rescue float, the kind lifeguards always carried. This he used mainly to smack his kayaking students playfully on the helmet if they neglected to get something right.

They both watched as Sky gave step-by-step directions on rolling the boat to the first two volunteers. There were several blue off spring who could roll beautifully, having spent time with Julian on his surfing waves, but also taking up the sport on their own, too. A surprising number of mothers wanted to come. This meant five mothers in all, but there were two very highly regarded world-class kayakers related to other blues who signed on, so the trip would be interesting. Beryl and Royal had desperately wanted a turn in Sky's old beginner boat, so Julian let them have it and a paddle, but no spray skirt in the shallow end of the enormous pool where they could practice tipping over and bailing out without bothering the others.

Uninterested in the whole affair, Julia was off with Rini for her turn on the sewing machine. Rini had informed Julian that she had organized her suture and first aid kits just in case she had to sew up any wounds, and had promised to keep her phone in her pocket should such an emergency arise. Since Beryl, Royal and Sky were there, Sunday would not leave her seat at the table under the umbrella. Water terrified her, and watching the boys tip upside down in the boat, caused her to begin a deep, prolonged wail with all eight fingers stuffed in her mouth. No one could lure her either into the water or away from it. Both Mars and Julian had tried to get her to stand next to them and hold their hand, but she would not go near the edge of the pool even with all of her floating devices secured to her small body.

Eventually, Soulful came down the walk, keeping in the shade of the trees to sit next to her. "Hey there, little sister, come on now. Nothing is going to happen to them. I mean, I don't like the water either, but you don't think Dad or Grey is going to let anything happen to your brothers do you?" She scooted her chair closer to his, took his hand, and wailed a little softer. Julian had given up on trying to console her, the fear was too primal, and Rini said to leave her be until she could come to the pool to get her. Cloris was at a nearby spa doing whatever it was women did in those mysterious places.

The same gardeners that maintained his last house kept the grounds there only now. They came early to have coffee with whoever was out. During their lunch break, the gardeners had turned off all the power cleaning machines to stand near the pool and watch the kids trying to get the boats flipped over, first upside down, then right side up. Someone had brought them beer. The melodramatic Mexican songs began to pour out of their ever-present boom box. The men started deciding who had it and who didn't, in the way that men make everything a contest, taking sides, laying small bets. The atmosphere was beginning to feel festive. Julian waved at them as he walked over to speak with Soulful.

"How's the sun shining for you, Soulful?" Julian said, giving Sunday a pat on the back, her smile glimmered. "I don't want a turn," she said.

"You are not permitted in the water today, Sunday. The pool is closed to all swimming lessons. So do not beg me to put you in there," Julian said firmly. Her shoulders relaxed a little, but her fingers went back into her mouth.

Soulful leaned toward Julian, "I can't find a DNA test for the white one."

"I think we should try a different code name for Lane," Julian said, making Soulful laugh.

"Okay how about *Lame*?" Soulful suggested.

Julian shook his head. "Just say Lane."

"Listen Julian, two things: he's been in and out of rehab and hospitals. He's up to something, and not broke either so it isn't money. He was adopted by her husband when he was a baby. He's not an attorney and he's not a lobbyist or whatever he tried to tell you. Naomi said to leave his story to her, also not to trust him."

"She says that about everyone. And the second thing?" Julian asked. Soulful got up and walked out of Sunday's hearing range, so Julian followed. Even past the newly planted shade tree he put his head to his and whispered. "Julia's mother has been trying to contact her again. She's pretty slick with the computer. I'm just giving you information. Rini said to see her about something that occurred when they were out shopping for fabric."

"She can't have contact of any kind. Julia knows nothing about her, but that woman is deranged. In the future Rini will need to take someone with her. I'll call the police," Julian confided only that much to give Soulful an understanding of the relationship. "I feel like we are under some kind of attack."

"Not attack precisely, more like close scrutiny," Soulful said, making Julian laugh.

"All this for being blue. Well put. Are you coming on the trip?"

"I can't decide. I want to go, but I also want to stay here and keep after things."

"We have an entire security company for that. And Naomi, too. I would love you to come," Julian said.

"I worry," Soulful said.

"Me, too," said Julian.

The security company was already there to see about providing more privacy. Soulful and Julian discussed the plan so far. More nets were going up, but these were the rather invisible kind, to try and catch the irritating flying spy-cameras, those tiny busy drones, much like a spider catches a flying insect. Now that Julian saw the drones, he could not ignore them. They were planting more trees, and putting up more porticos. The idea of trying to shield their privacy from the American government shocked Julian, but he could not ignore the facts. Somehow this estate was viewed as some sort of compound, and their color made them suspect for being some type of separate nation. Soulful and Julian discussed this as well.

"Technology gets developed, people just believe that it's come to humankind to use it. Like the gift of fire, kind of," Soulful said.

"Please really consider coming. You would be a great team member, maybe even critical to the group," Julian said.

"Think so?" Soulful asked, but this time much more like he was really considering it.

"How about this. You come along and I'll arrange for the two of us to spend a couple of days caving while they start their practice runs on the American River. See what you can find for us in central California. And you can show me what you like about caves."

"Seriously?" Soulful asked.

"Get the equipment organized and let me know what I need," Julian answered.

Grey Mars blew his whistle, getting Julian's attention.

The two younger boys had come up with a contest that involved Beryl standing on the bow while Royal jumped on the stern from the edge of the pool. Beryl landed flat on his back on an occupied kayak, tipping it over to many screams of indignation.

"Get out, and wait your turn with your sister Sunday," Julian ordered. As always, they first looked stunned to find themselves doing such a thing and then obeyed without being told twice. Sunday's whine stopped as soon as the boys exited the pool, she called to them, "Roy, Ber, how was it?" like she was getting ready to go next. There was no way the small children were going camping with them this time. Julian would make it up to them some other way, this reminded him to consult with Cloris and Rini about suitable sitters.

Julian turned his attention back to the pool, the two kayaks, his determined blue teenagers leaning the boats on their edge trying to angle the paddle for that perfect set up before the roll over. Everyone was properly fitted into life jackets, which were always called *PFD*s, and snug helmets. Sky was in her own boat ready to demonstrate on Mars's command. She smiled and waved a gloved hand at Julian who waved back instantly.

"The rule is you stay in the boat on the river. You're safer, we're all safer. Bailing out is the absolute last resort. Watch Sky set up and roll. Notice her head is always down and her body is rolling over the back of the boat. When she sets up she pushes the paddle clear of the water." Sky snapped up a perfect roll. After several fails, someone suggested that there was probably a more Zen way to teach rolling the boat. When Mars heard this he slapped both hands over his heart and pretended to be shot dead. "You gotta use your hips, keep your head down by pushing out of the water shoulder first and *roll* up. There ain't no Zen about it. You roll your body. It's a *combat* roll, and it needs to be bombproof, into muscle memory. When you flip the water is going to be turbulent, not a swimming pool." Julian knew Mars was keeping his language clean because of the smaller children there. His boys were spending the week with their mother, which meant they were in summer camp and Mars would pick them up each evening at six.

For perhaps the hundredth time Mars went through his mini lecture: the trick was for a right side roll the right knee was quickly pulled toward the chest while the left hip dropped. The head had to roll back and stay down. It was a quick, hard snap in this flat, still water. Mars went over this time and again patiently.

"Now one at a time," Mars yelled.

Two boats rolled over at the same time, Indigo and Li-Si, the two most competitive and tireless students in the pool that morning. When Li-Si first declared she would be going along, Julian worried, but Mars convinced him to at least let her try to learn the basics see if that would scare her off. So far, it had not, if anything it made her easier to deal with.

Both boats were bottom up for a minute, both paddles were in the right position, both men held their breath. One pair of blue hands ratcheted the paddle and popped up the roll. A triumphant Indigo smiled, but when the second boat stayed upside down and the hands disappeared freeing the paddle to float on the surface, but no Li-Si swam out, Julian dove in, colliding with Mars under water. They both pulled the bail cord and popped out the Li-Si who flipped to the surface in one flash of shimmering purple.

Once everyone was breathing air, Julian said, "Okay. Excellent effort, you didn't panic. Good breath control. Dump out the boat, let's try again."

But Mars, his thinning hair plastered to his head like a shredded swim cap, pulled Li-Si aside by the elbow. "Look kiddo, you can't let yourself drown. If you miss the roll, and can't get it wedged up enough to get some air, get the fuck out of that boat right now. We'll cover this more when we're on the river next week and things are moving, but you be confident that if you have to bail, we will be right behind you to help you out of the river and back into your boat? Okay? You get three set ups to try to hit your roll and then bail. That scared ten years off of me. When you get back in, we are going to set up your roll and help you through step by step until you get it."

"Yes, sir. I'm ready to do it a thousand times until I am ready for this trip," she answered in the most humble voice Julian had ever heard spoken from her glossed lips. So that was how she got to the top, being who she had to be and working hard, he thought a bit proudly. After lifting Mars's hat from the surface of the water and flying it to his open palm, Julian toweled off his face, confident the sun would dry him completely within fifteen minutes.

All in all, Julian felt confident the group would have a great time, and no one would get seriously hurt. Next, they would take the boats to the ocean surf, probably San Onofre, where kayakers often went to play in the surf, and practice rolling. After that they would spend ten days on the American River practicing. Julian felt he had corralled the energy, and had things in hand once again. Those who weren't willing to participate were already leaving for other parts to spend the rest of the summer. Julian made it clear they were welcome back for short visits, but only when he was there. Security was reinforced.

"Pa!"

Julian recognized Tauro's voice immediately. Also, he was the only off spring to call him Pa, and he turned around smiling. There was Tauro, flexing his enormous muscles, wearing his favorite t-shirt that stated: *Fine China Blue* in script.

"I'm here with my Mom. We're going on the kayak trip," he said. The woman that stepped from behind Tauro had skin so black it shimmered blue in the intense southern California sunlight. Tall, and long-necked, with her hair wrapped in a brilliant headband, Julian estimated she was at least six inches taller than he was.

"My name is Elita. Julian, I have been dying to meet you," she said smiling just like her son. As Julian had always imagined she was solid muscle on bone, with an extraordinary face.

Grey Mars blew his whistle, and Julian waved him off, going directly to Tauro's mother, his hand outstretched, his stride so quick he was almost hopping. Their fingertips touched first, but when he noticed his embarrassing blue hand next to her beautiful ebony, he almost drew it back, almost apologized, but she grabbed him to her with the same strength of her son, pulling him into a hug just as hard.

"You feel good!" She announced gently rubbing his back.

"I do?" Julian replied, making her laugh. He liked her pearly, crooked teeth, the way she wrapped her hair with a colorful batik scarf, the black curls springing out.

"I could hug you again to double check!" She laughed. Julian started to step in for another, but already Sunday, Royal and Beryl were there, trying to wedge their way between them. Tauro lifted Sunday over his head and spun her around, making her laugh.

"Hey cry baby, you learned to swim yet?"

"Not yet!" she squealed.

Elita tugged Julian's hand. "I speak Spanish so I can help navigate Mexico. It's my first language. My family is from the Dominican Republic, but I know Mexico very well. I used to volunteer down there in the clinic. I'm strong, and a doctor, too. So I can look after you. I brought my kit," Elita told Julian.

"Are you going to kayak?" He asked already imagining himself in the pool guiding her through the steps.

"No, I'm going to keep you all safe," she declared making Tauro laugh his great, round laugh.

Grey Mars blew and blew his whistle, until Julian reluctantly turned around.

"I'm feeling left out over here!" Mars shouted. The kids in the pool stopped what they were doing to see what the commotion was about. Everyone, but Mars went back to setting up and flipping the boats. They were on their own now, Mars's was on his way over, dropping his lifeguard float on the way. No one could accuse either man of not dropping everything to meet a beautiful woman.

Seemingly from behind one of the newly planted clumps of trees Rini was there to collect Sunday, with Julia in hand—Julian really had no idea how long she'd been watching, but she went straight to Elita. "Well, if you aren't the thunder clap I've been praying for!" She told her, clasping her hands together over her heart, her face tipped to the sky in the way she expressed gratitude. Although with her strong accent that always got thicker when she got excited, he couldn't be exactly sure if that is what she said, but it made Elita collect her into her big hug. Julian patted the heads that surrounded him, but pretended her was studying Elita to look for the similarities in Tauro.

"You do look thunder-struck," Mars said into Julian's ear.

"I have no idea what that expression means," Julian replied.

"Yes you do," Mars said chuckling, but fortunately keeping the wild hyena laugh in.

After that Julian only got fleeting glimpses of Elita, even though it seemed like every molecule in his blue body was searching her out.

One morning as he was preparing the house for the first trip to kayak on the American River as a group, she surprised him.

"Where do all the teenagers sleep? I saw how you have that dorm with those unique built in unique beds, like cupboards, like the Europeans, with lamps, book shelves, but mostly they are empty, and still made."

"That was an inspiration from Rini. When we were planning the house," Julian said, trying to sound collected, and natural.

"I like her. She knows this world," Elita said.

"For some reason the older kids prefer to sleep outside, under the porticos and the trees. There's bedrooms, beds, more comfort. Of course if they aren't going on the trip, they have to go home. That's the rule. Of course, I have the four young ones. They get to stay. And Sky and Soulful." He babbled about the satellite problems, the other instances of civil disobedience.

"Maybe rebelling is what the young are supposed to do, but not until they can afford to support themselves. House rules," Elita said simply. "So Rini did tell me about your four little ones. That says a lot about you Julian. My son told me you were a good man."

"Well," Julian said, embarrassed. "Tauro has told me so much about you that I feel like we are already friends. But, he would never have had to say a word for me to know what a great mother you are."

That brought on a long awkward moment of silently eyeing each other up and down. Julian, embarrassed as always about his color, turned away. Elita walked silently back the way she came. If only he could casually ask Rini where she had stationed Elita's guest quarters without Rini doing some form of mazurka in quadruple meter around him, he would.

The next time he caught a glimpse of her he was outside trying to motivate Royal and Beryl into leaving the colorful computer screens for some sunshine.

"There's no one to take us swimming?" they asked. Julian had the pool enclosed in it's own tall wrought iron structure with several locking gates. The point was to keep the young ones out for their own safety.

As a child he had the forest, streams, mountains, but besides, skis, a sled and ice skates, no toys, not even a dog.

"Just play!" Julian waved to the vast grounds, exasperated. That was the second time he saw Elita wrapped in a brilliant dress, against her black skin waving at them.

"Wait up!" she called, her voice sounding like a young girl's. Julian wondered where she grew up, and decided to ask her if he could work it in.

When she caught up with them, she hugged the boys, ruffled their hair, asked what they were up to. Julian thought her accent was the most perfect American pronunciation of vowels. He would never tire of hearing it.

"Playing outside," they answered so politely no one could miss their desperation to get out of it.

"And you Julian?"

"I have been thinking of installing a petite orchard of different varieties of fig trees." This was what he began thinking about as soon as it was decided to plant more trees.

"Figs?"

The tone left him fumbling for words. "Yes, I thought they were interesting. We saw a kind of collection of fig trees in a recent trip to a botanical garden. Do you remember that boys?"

Before they could answer a sprinkler went off between Julian's legs.

Beryl and Royal exploded in laughter as they ran alongside of Elita to get away from the spray.

"You need a towel," Elita declared, her laughter still rumbling from deep inside. He was pleased to make her laugh, but also too embarrassed to laugh at himself like he would have had it been anyone else standing there.

"Let me go get one," she said trying to keep her voice even.

"I'll dry off in a few minutes," Julian said, slowly regaining his dignity.

"So tomorrow we're all going to the river! Are you boys going too?" Elita said.

"Not this time. They are still too young," Julian said. "They will have plenty to do here. Next year they'll get their start. This summer its violin lessons, science camp and learning to write apps on the computer."

"We do want to go though," Royal said. Julian patted the top of his head.

"Don't worry boys, I'll keep my eye on your father. And Julian, I've decided to try a little kayaking, in the beginner-beginner's class," Elita said. She meant their practice runs on the American River, a long ten-hour drive away. Mars had arranged for skill-leveled classes with two kayaking outfits up there.

"I'm glad to hear it. I'll be there a day or two following the group. Soulful and I are going caving, before we join the rest of you at the campground," he told Elita as he tried to rake his hair into shape without flinging any water droplets onto her.

"We're going to really miss you," Royal said. Julian hoped he meant it.

Elita took a half step toward Julian to whisper, "I came to ask your permission for something. Yesterday, I promised to take

Tauro shopping with Julia, Sunday, and Rini. Do you think that is okay? Rini told me about the incident with that hair pulling."

"I'll have someone else go along, too," Julian said, finally feeling authoritative.

They spent another few seconds eyeing each other silently before each turning to go in the opposite direction.

"She waved at us! Wave, Beryl!" Royal reported. Julian didn't turn around, but he did smile.

That evening Naomi called. "Listen, Jules, I only have a minute sorry to be so abrupt, it's my kids thing happening here, and I'm waiting my turn to take some pics, but keep that Lane character at a distance. I'm not sure he's related to you. He's pretty cagey."

"What do you think he wants?" Julian asked.

"Jules, I think he wants a kidney. Oh shit, sorry, it's my turn, gotta go."

Julian kept the phone to his ear a full minute after the call went off, like he was

trying to still hear what had been said.

# Chapter Fourteen

The day everyone was ready to set off for the American river, the adults were having a final pow-wow in the meticulously planned room that Cloris called the comfortable den. This meant twenty people could sit comfortably in it and put their feet on the furniture because of something she called washable slipcovers, and distressed hardwood finishes; the furnishings eclectic, the colors passive. Earlier Cloris had told the women that the carefully controlled palette had no less than eleven shades of white. Mars and Julian still privately joked about her designer expressions over beers, though the subject of color was still a touchy one for Julian even after all these years he had to agree with Mars that an entire sitcom could be written around Cloris, the devoted decorator (No! No! Too perfect, too matchy. That pillow offends everything in its surroundings, which was pure until now. It's spoilt. No! No! That is not straight, not balanced.) This was probably the second time Julian had gone inside the room. The women all entered the room marveling at what they called its relaxing subtlety, comparing it often to that mythical woman's nirvana, the spa. Naturally Mars leapt at his chance to become the center of attention with the women, and began to seriously describe the thoughtful décor, letting the hungry hyena laugh out so often they finally stopped leaping away in surprise each time, adapting to Mars's unique charm. It helped that he was obviously rich, generous, and a great and caring father. Cloris, who also adored Mars, helped pump up the myths. The laws of the jungle, Julian supposed.

Julian was glad that Cloris was busy supervising Sky's packing. That morning as soon as Julian got up Sky began a loud, rambling protest, something like a nonsensical filibuster, really, trying to keep Julian from going caving with Soulful. "You are trying to replace me with a son." Sky wailed. Those trying teenage years sharpened her skills for offering indefensible arguments. Fortunately for Julian, Cloris had arrived early to help with the mothers, and swiftly came to Julian's rescue. "Shut that voice off Miss Sky, right now, or you can stay here with me and help us care for the little dolls." Sky obeyed, but after that she effectively replaced her words by slamming and rattling everything that could be moved. The little dolls, all the younger children staying behind scuttled to the safety of Rini's part of the house.

The younger children took his leaving, like everything else, stoically and without protest, but it secretly gratified Julian that when he bent down to them, they hugged him hard and cried silently on his shoulder. Rini had taken them, and Mars's two boys with her to the airport to pick up her daughter. The kids were going to have an exclusive summer camp of sorts while the adults were gone. Now exhausted from the goodbyes, all Julian wanted to do was escape the comfortable den quickly and quietly.

"Ready?" he asked Soulful, who in response shouldered his backpack, and pocketed his ever-present cell phone.

Before they got out the door, Grey Mars pulled Soulful back.

"Soul, there are some things you gotta know about Julian and caves," he said without changing the volume of his voice. In his defense, he only really had two volumes, speaking and snoring, both loud.

"Grey," Julian said, trying to communicate in that one syllable that he had already spoken to Soulful about his cave fugues, but the other moms were watching now and Grey Mars would always play to the feminine crowd.

"I think I should hear this," Soulful said quietly.

"All I'm trying to say is that if Julian goes into this zombie mode and begins to drift towards, oh say, a cliff or a bottomless pit, or a surging typhoon of certain death you're gonna have to physically stop him. It's like sleep walking of the highest level," Grey said this so seriously that everyone's mouth fell open. For the first time since they had all gathered in there, the room went quiet. This was followed by inner-circle glances and then the, "Maybe this isn't such a good idea, Julian." And on like that. All this chatter flustered Julian who was already overwhelmed with these capable, smart, good-natured women, ready to take over the world. Just when he was feeling grateful that Elita was not there to hear it all, she stepped into the room.

"Women, we are going to need help outside with packing the camping gear." Elita called out lifting her brow at Julian. He hoped his slight nod communicated his unbroken interest in her. For some reason, Julian and Elita had stopped deliberately seeking each other's company and were now in some sort of circling game. Now they took in each other with slicing glances: just happening to be there as each turned a corner, or entering the room, just as the other was leaving. It more than slightly rankled Julian that Mars and Tauro had taught her to roll the kayak without him, almost secretly, but that had to be her decision. In spite of himself, Julian smiled at her, probably looking desperately goofy.

Thankfully, the women stood and followed without asking for any further explanation. Julian tried to watch Elita lead them out, but all he caught was a flash of her brilliant green dress leaving the room.

"That was something," Mars commented.

"Amazing," Julian responded, keeping the sour look off his face.

"Now back to what I was saying," Mars said.

"These are more caverns than caves," Soulful said to Mars, leaving out the part that they had arranged to go on a special tour inside another part of the caverns with an expert from the park service in which their height and weight had to fall under a certain level in order to fit through the passages. Small spaces wasn't the part that worried Julian.

"Dad!" Sky called just as they were getting into the car. "Dad, wait!" She ran to him, wrapped her arms around him. "I'm sorry. Have all the fun you can with Soulful. I'm sorry I was behaving so badly. I'll see you on the river."

"See you on the river," Julian repeated. And then she waved, and left, freeing him.

"Take care of Dad," Sky sternly told Soulful who shrugged, as if to say, okay, why not?

Soulful was driving the first shift. After he got the car started he said, "That Sky is one tough girl, like Cloris. She's on my Zombie Defense Team."

"Zombie Defense Team?"

"It's a game we have among the Blues, and others, too. Zombies are pretty popular this decade," Soulful said, teasing him.

"Zombies," Julian repeated, "Did Grey just compare me to one?"

"Don't worry, he didn't mean he thought you would be eating my brains," Soulful said.

"I know what he meant," Julian said, but he was thinking about something else. He was thinking about telling Soulful all he could remember about that fateful blue-turning kayak trip, the pink lake, everything, just in case. Even the details he never told anyone before. Soulful asked if he could record the history, maybe put it together with the footage that was taken during that trip.

"You have to be very careful," Julian said. "That part of the world is very fragile."

"Okay," Soulful said. And Julian told him everything he could remember even making him laugh when he told him about the group running for their lives from the tiny natives slicing at them with their sharp knives.

"The guides insisted that we had to call in their location and that we had some contact," Julian recalled. "In case we gave them a germ that would wipe them out. I remember the guide using that satellite phone. I'm pretty sure they did a fly over very shortly after that."

"I think we could locate that lake. If you wanted a water sample or something. If it would help you to, you know, satisfy your curiosity. I hesitate to say, get closure because it's one of my mom's favorite sayings and I've learned there's no such thing," Soulful said.

They had decided to drive through for food and gas, stopping only when they got to the hotel, only because their timeline was so tight. There was a yellow and red drive through, called *In and Out* that Soulful particularly favored. Julian found himself deliberately searching for them as they rolled along.

When Soulful said, "Are you getting hungry?" Julian was ready.

They swooped in on the next one Julian spotted, drove through and ordered what they had every time before with NO ONIONS, almost a sacrilege in that place, Soulful laughed. Julian marveled that each restaurant not only looked identical to its relatives along the highway, but the taste and texture of the food never varied either. While they sat in the car and ate, Soulful asked Julian more questions about that fateful kayaking trip, and then about Lana.

"Back then it seemed like we spent a lot of time together at events and things, although I barely knew her we did spend the night together a few times. If you want to succeed in anything, you have to be ambitious, and she was ambitious, almost in a predatory way. She's the reason we went on that first trip, but I told you this, I think."

Julian expected Soulful to bring up Lane again, but instead he stuffed his trash into the paper bag and asked, "Have you ever been in love?"

He was going to snap off his usual, "no," but Julian thought about Elita, how her skin was the color of the smooth black river rock that he kept at his bedside and rolled in his palm when he was deeply thinking. From there his thoughts skipped over to that smooth hub of her shoulder, her scent, the way her earrings swung so freely from the lobes. He never let his mind travel to more Southerly parts. Julian carefully blocked his sexual desire for her because he did not want the frustration of never having her, something he was certain he would never get over.

"I'm not sure," Julian said carefully sipping the hot coffee. "Have you ever been in love?"

"Yes. Once. That's when I first contacted you. She was great, her parents were okay with me, I mean they weren't people who saw color, they thought I had enough going for me to qualify. My mom was thrilled, probably relieved I wasn't gay, both her brothers are, and she thinks they are too emotional, too draining. Her words. I was only sixteen. I had already graduated from high school. I got accepted to Yale, my first choice. I had to get out of there. It all seemed so life threatening back then."

Julian laughed so suddenly he spit coffee onto the windshield. This made Soulful laugh, too. When they finally stopped, Julian said, "You are going to go to Yale?"

"No way. I'm going to UCLA. Like you. I just got accepted, in pre-med. Please do not tell my mother, she will never let me hear the end of it," Soulful said. The rest of the drive they took in a comfortable silence watching the farmland open into that golden grassy undulating land, like lions fur. Mark Twain's gold country. There were many small rivers, but because of the statewide drought, many dry-river-beds, something Julian found immeasurably depressing. Still, he envied the people who lived in this gently forested land, the broad fenced farms dotted with cows on the free range, horses in generous pens and even goats in much smaller enclosures, kicking up their heels, or doing as all the other animals did: chewed on the vegetation. Because of the drought many growers had to get their own wells dug, Julian remembered reading. Here and there corn grew in thick rows, and the sight of the orchards of fruit and nut trees seemed to redefine Eden, in his mind. After ten hours of driving, they checked into a hotel so the next morning they would be rested and ready for the long day. That night they would stay in another hotel so they would be on the American River in early morning, again rested and ready. Julian looked forward to that.

The guide, dressed in a muddy green, one-piece mechanic's suit with an oval patch embroidered with the name Cliff, met them outside the small gift shop. "My name tag says Cliff, but my name is really Jake." He told them in such a joking way, Julian wondered which was his real name.

After that Cliff/Jake advised them on what to expect in a fairly, monotone spiel that made Julian rather pity him his job. The three shook hands as they went through brief introductions. Cliff/Jake's handshake was strong, almost crushing. Because Julian was so self-conscious about other people's reaction to his color, it took several minutes before he could look directly at the guide. Cliff/Jake was much older than Julian had first thought, and his green eyes blazed with intelligence. He hadn't shaved in a day or so. The beginnings of silvery whiskers followed the contours of his face, wrinkles, cleft in his chin.

"Let me go put the releases away, and grab a couple of things. You said you brought your own gear? You can go change over there," the guide said, disappearing inside the adjacent shack.

They went to a rudimentary dressing area built with unvarnished two-by-fours, plywood, and gigantic nails, but no cover from the penetrating sun. Soulful pulled open his gear bag, saying, "They will provide this stuff but I read online that it's pretty tattered so I brought what we need: helmets, coveralls, gloves, and boots. Of course we'll wear our own boots. Flat flashlights, lighter, matches."

Julian looked everything over, stupidly grateful that the coveralls were dark blue and not bright orange as he had seen in the brochures.

"I put a camera on one of the helmets. What do you think?" Soulful asked.

"I think you've thought of everything," Julian said.

The guide appeared again and began talking as they pulled the cover alls over their jeans and t-shirts. Cave mud was sticky and would stain everything they were wearing, they would get dripped on, fall in water, and crawl through passages of dead zones, no light, where sterile water flowed through the cavern, there was very little life other than chilly air. Some passages were a body-leg, brace crawl press where most people ended up in the water. Many they would have to go in on their side and work themselves around narrow passages.

Julian's mood felt grimmer by the minute, so he had to use his full acting talents to appear relaxed and looking forward to voluntarily interning himself under the ground, alive.

There would be an opportunity to repel into a second cavern if they felt up to it. Julian and Soulful both agreed they would be up for it. This time he wasn't acting. Afterward there would be showers.

"There are some places that are going to require going a few feet by touch alone. Some areas we'll have to remove the muddy gloves so that we don't spread it," he told them.

Julian began massaging his fingertips with the pads of his thumb. No calluses, he would probably get blisters walking them over the rough surfaces. When had he become so soft?

"You going to be okay in there?" Soulful asked.

"I'm ready, and I'm glad I came. Stop worrying," Julian said, following their guide to some sort of hobbled together staging area made of stacked rocks and yellowed weeds. "We're ready." Julian told the guide.

The guide broke character at this point and turned to Julian to tell him how much he loved his Aqua Man movies, would he be making any more? Julian explained his retirement, how his involvement with young children took up most of his time, leaving out the part that he did practically nothing towards raising them except provide them with blue skin, his name, bed and board and his time, most of which was spent inside his own mind trying to translate children's speech into something comprehensible, a task he never felt equal to. Around the smaller ones, he was always

146

very careful to never say yes to anything until he was certain he understood or got the nod from Cloris or Rini. Mainly Julian worked full time keeping track of his money, something he would never say out loud. Placing a hand over his heart, he realized he missed his young children. Julian thought he had finally reached some sort of milestone in his life, as if now he was ready to be a real person.

The inquisitive guide asked if it had been hard to leave acting.

"It made me blue," Julian answered deadpan. "And now I want your job. That's why we've come. To study you," Julian added. Soulful's laugh barked out; he quickly apologized for letting it escape.

"Oh come on, you can fine me funny," Julian pretended to scold him.

"Well, being studied by a famous actor would be the most interesting thing that's happened to me in years," Cliff/Jake said cheerfully. And then the guide looked around like he wanted to be certain he wasn't going to be overheard. When he crouched down so did Soulful so then Julian had to, too. Their three heads drew to the center.

"Listen, I have a different section we can explore. It was discovered in the late 1950s, and has never been open to the public. It's pretty strenuous. I go in to get samples, something I need to do right now. Want to go take a look? Help collect some samples? I have to swear you to secrecy. There is a beautiful pond down there. The cavern is so far below the local groundwater water table it's still two feet deep this time of year. In the wet season, if we ever have one again, it completely floods and can't be safely accessed. We'll exit out a hidden spot, too, so we can avoid everyone else. You'll have to turn the camera off when I ask. Whad'da ya think?"

"Hell yes!" Soulful cried, and inwardly Julian shuddered, but pretended to match Soulful's enthusiasm.

"Do you want us to leave the camera behind?" Julian asked.

"No. I trust you Julian. I'll let you know when filming isn't prudent."

"I'll turn the camera off," Soulful said. "We don't need it."

"We ready?"

"We'll keep my dad between the two of us," Soulful told the guide when they were lining up to go into the first squeeze.

"Okay then," he said cheerfully. "Julian if you get claustrophobic, just let me know, we can back out and take other passages."

"It's not claustrophobia," Julian said stubbornly, and without trying to elaborate.

"The native Indians believed it their spirits lived in the caves, so they never entered them," the guide said, like he might have some inkling about Julian's cave fugues.

"But not because of claustrophobia," Julian said.

"Not according to myth," the guide answered.

"So it's a rather universal concept then."

This observation was greeted with silence, so Julian tied on the headscarf in the same way Soulful did, tested the light and fit the helmet snugly to his head by turning the convenient knob on the back. Apparently Soulful intended for Julian to wear the camera.

"So I'm not going to point out features and compare them to what you might imagine they can be. Like that looks like a bear, the budda, or a wedding cake. We'll talk geology, and caving. How's that?"

"I think that's why we came," Soulful said.

"No one has ever died in here," the guide told Julian. When he turned to lead them, Julian secretly swallowed a Xanax and followed his small team through the gentle, wooded path. While Soulful and Cliff/Jake exchanged cave information, Julian pictured Rini, the children, wondered what Cloris was changing, Mars would keep Sky safe, he didn't worry about her, but mostly he thought of Elita, her son.

"Solutional caves are the most frequently occurring caves. They form in rock that is soluble, such as limestone, but can also form in other rocks. Over time the rock is dissolved by the natural acid in groundwater that seeps through what you might think of as the floor. Cracks form, water fills in, and so it goes over very long geological epochs, those cracks expand to become caves and cave systems.

The largest and most abundant solutional caves are located

in limestone. Limestone dissolves under the action of rainwater and groundwater charged with carbonic acid and naturally occurring organic acids. Limestone caves, like this one, are often adorned with calcium carbonate formations produced through slow precipitation. These include flowstones, stalactites, stalagmites, helictites, soda straws and columns. All those forms we guides like to relate to ridiculous cartoon characters and such for the tourists entertainment. They are wonders without being compared to anything in so called normal life."

"So what are speleothems?" Soulful asked.

"Those are secondary mineral deposits."

In Julian's experience, caves came in a surprising array of forms, materials and sizes. He told Soulful and the guide about exploring ice caves when he was a child, which was a slight exaggeration, as he usually accidentally fell, or stumbled into them. He did not mention his last experience with a cave, which was a mine so he wasn't sure if it counted anyway. If Soulful knew the story of his deranged father, he never asked about it.

"Do you miss Norway?" the guide asked, catching Julian off guard.

"Of course," Julian said. He often thought of Norway, there was no place in the world like it, but he knew he never needed to go back there. What he missed was his own home, his oddly cobbled together family, full of sunshine.

"Which part of Norway are you from?" the guide asked.

"Troms, Norway. It's very north, remote, and so very different than Oslo, or anywhere you might see in pictures. At least it was then. I haven't been back in so many years," Julian said.

"Would I like to visit there?" Soulful asked.

"You would love it," Julian said feeling his knees soften. And because he could not ignore Soulful's questions, Julian found himself describing his homeland, as he remembered from his lonely boyhood. Looking back, he supposed that's when his mind began turning itself over to Trom, that past, in what would become an avalanche of memories once he was encased in the earth.

The way into the cave was a metal door built into a hillside. Once it was opened, it was obvious this had been carefully constructed for many tourists to enter, and follow a rough, muddy path with a primitive guardrail through the cavern. There was a large group already gathered, all peering up at the ceiling, which was made up of dripping mud-scicles. The place moaned, but that was mainly from the children wanting something more amusing than the slick narrow pathway, the damp, smelly earth, and walls that looked like dirty melted ice cream. The guide led them quietly down a very dark passage. From there they slid through a hidden opening in a rock, Soulful waited for Julian to enter, and their journey into the slippery, primitive darkness began.

*Stalactites hold tight to the ceiling. Stalagmites might make it from the floor to the top. Three light sources are essential. Never reach for glowing eyes. The first explorers got lost for eight days when they lost their light source. Always carry three light sources. Let's see how far we can crawl in the total black. Call out the word 'light' when you've had enough.*

*Spring, he was home, his mother had not appeared Julian crawled on his hands and knees into the tight niche in the side of the earth, when he emerged, he was a bear walking on his hind legs, pawing at the air, growling. The dense wet air was like the water, a liquid turquoise. The wild grass a carpet of lime green, the grey stones looked like the hills. It wasn't until he stepped into the freezing water did he realize his brain had somehow reinvented the world. Julian stood at the bank trying to decide whether to just keep moving into the water or turn toward home. And then there was his mother, wrapping him in a wool blanket. "I warned you," she whispered. "Stay away from these parts they are harmful beings here." Julian wanted to break her grasp, wrest free. When he looked into her face, her blue face. Blue face, blue hands. "Don't be afraid. I am just like my sisters now," she whispered, but he would not take her glowing hand.*

"Light!" Julian called, surrendering first. The dim headlight ahead of him came on immediately. The pupils of his eyes gratefully responded, his brain let go of some type of endorphins that made Julian feel a tingle of relief in every muscle of his body. Somehow he got his own light turned on.

"You okay Soul?"

"I'm good. Why, could you hear my heart hammering?"

Julian could tell by his son's soft, even breathing that he had been and still was completely relaxed in the total blackness in which Julian had mentally flailed.

"If you get that feeling you are floating in space, just use your flat palms against the wall to anchor yourself. Think: I can go one more inch," the guide said. They were wedged against the rough wall.

"The dark just drives my mind inward. There is no sense of here now," Julian whispered, but he now felt confident that he would be able to stay focused.

"Feel the updraft of air?" The guide asked. He was talking to Soulful, now that Julian was mostly silent, turning the image of his mother over and over in his mind, wondering about the hallucination. There were rumors, whispers, but also paintings, and the blue dolls his mother sewed to keep around her bed like charms. Fish on her head, bird on her head, apron full of flowers, spear across her shoulder. All were sewn in some shade of blue fabric the hair from unraveled rope or yarn, maybe. "My sisters," she told him once when he pointed at one. Julian's carved blue box. "When you are feeling sad, open this box and look at the things you have collected inside. This will help you to remember who you are." Julian thought of little Julia and her pineapple obsession, Royal's small cars, Beryl's little plastic blue people, and Sunday's baskets of stuffed koalas.
"Soulful, do you have a collection of anything?"

There was a moment when both men exhaled with relief, silently communicating to Julian that he must have been acting very strange.

"All sane people have a collection of at least one thing. Looking at them gives you joy. It helps you to remember who you are," Soulful said, giving Julian chills to hear his mother's words from a grandson she never met.

"I like to collect several things," Soulful said. "Old books, pictures of clouds, things like that."

"I collect old tools," the guide offered. "Especially miner's small pick axes. Don't know why, I just love them. And the adze, probably the first real tool of humans, amazes me. Drives my wife nuts, so they have their own tool shed."

"What do you collect Julian?"

"Right now, blue off-spring. But I do have a rather serious collection of small stones that I have picked up at the places I've visited." He already had one in his pocket, it was the size of a licorice jellybean, smooth, and black. This was in the parking area, so who knows where it came from. This representation of Elita gave him a little thrill.

As he had promised the guide lead them through a final worm hole and then out into a hillside that looked upon a fenced pasture.

"Don't come out until I make sure no one is around," the guide said.

"You okay?" Soulful asked.

"I see sunlight," Julian laughed. "I can't remember the last time I was this hungry."

"Me, too," Soulful said. "We'll find a real restaurant and have four dishes and fresh fruit, ripe avocadoes. You can get a drink of alcohol. I'll drive."

"You're a good son, Soulful, and by that I mean not just a relative who serves, but a real, understanding friend," Julian said.

"So are you, and by that I mean not just a relative who gives, but my most important friend, too," he said. They both laughed.

When they got back the primitive staging area where they started, they made arrangements to explore another cave with the guide, another place he called legal to explore, but off the tourist grid, maybe after they got back from the kayak trip.

"Do you kayak?" Julian asked him.

"I'm an earth man. My theory is we are earth, water, or sky people. There might be some crossovers by adventure seekers, but there is always one strong preference each of us goes to when we need to settle down a flustered soul."

"Earth," Soulful said while Julian said, "Water."

In the small, primitive shower stall Julian rejoiced in the rusty smelling water that poured from the tap washing away the earth. The sun shined overhead, leaves from trees blew in. Being naked was the only time when Julian's blue skin did not bother him. In fact, the smooth, other worldly color did seem exotic and unbroken by the lines of clothes, natural in an exalted way. He called this thought over the shower stall to Soulful.

"You really wrestle with this, don't you?" Soulful called in his usual thoughtful, *how can I help make this easier for you?* tone. Sometimes Julian believed Soulful was there to look out for him and not the other way around. Maybe this was the way to be.

"Yes," Julian replied. "But, it's just that in the cave I had this thought, maybe it was a memory of my childhood in Norway. Anyway, I don't think the pink lake had anything to do with turning blue."

"Why, did your vision remind you of something?" Soulful asked with his usual candor, and acceptance.

"They are just warped dreams. Maybe wishes, ways to make things easier to think about," Julian said.

"Can you talk about it?"

"It was just a dream. Things that don't matter anymore," Julian whispered.

# Chapter Fifteen

"Let me out here at the store," Soulful instructed Julian after they had driven into the campground. "Don't wait, I'll walk over. I want to get some snacks. Stuff I know they won't have."

"I can't just leave you here just like that," Julian protested.

"Sure you can. I have a map of the campground, Julian. Grey emailed detailed directions. It's not far from here, like two blocks in city speak. Just go on ahead to the campsite. I'll be fine. Go on," Soulful instructed. Julian let him out, but he felt he was the one getting left.

A group of young men walked by in shorts and open shirts. One said, "how you doing man?" to Soulful who nodded in return. Another one signaled at Julian and then pointed left, like he would find his blue people that way. Julian did go that way noticing his blue off-spring everywhere. They all pointed in the direction he should follow. He had to admit those bright dots of color among the ordinary made him proud. He waved back as he rolled slowly down the road. People of all ages camped there, and almost every campsite had several tents, a wash line of drying paddle clothes, and a stack of kayaks. Julian relaxed.

Perhaps it was the true sign of his character, but when he parked in the campground, and made his way to the campsite, he looked not for Sky or even Grey Mars, but for the black skin of Elita.

Grey found him first. "Juli! We've taken over the place. Look at us. Over one hundred, give or take. When someone leaves we get another spot and spread out a little more. Some are rafting. The people here are very cool. We should've brought all the kids. Everyone from this community has integrated us. We should buy a second house here." The hungry hyena laugh assailed the clear warm, dry air.

Julian laughed, too. In his way, Mars really thought of himself as blue, too.

"It is beautiful here," Julian said trying not to be obvious in his search for the bright sundress, the big hats, that midnight skin.

"Elita is taking a shower just now," Grey Mars confided, pointing in the general direction of the building. "She's asked me about a thousand questions about you. She is trying to get good enough to kayak alongside you. That's a secret, by the way. My suggestion is you two stick to the Coloma to Lotus run, maybe Greenwood. She's confident and will roll, but man she flips a lot."

Julian smiled, smacked Grey Mars on the shoulder, who on contact, let out the hungry hyena.

"Let's try her in a different boat," Julian suggested. "Who are all the other teenagers?" He meant the non-blue ones squeezed in among his.

"Oh come on Julian, you don't think these teens are going to have this kind of fun without their friends? I didn't see any harm in letting them invite their significant others. So far, we've had no problems and absolutely no booze allowed. As a group, they don't seem to want to drink. No one can cook gourmet camp food, so we've been eating lots of oatmeal, hotdogs, pizza from the outside, chips, salads, sandwiches, and a lot of boiled eggs, cereal, milk. Fresh fruit, juice. Can't kill us right?"

"Who killed what?" Julian asked, waving to everyone that was waving at him, as he scanned for Elita possibly wrapped in a towel. He tried to walk as casually as he could. Mars let out the hungry hyena, causing other campers to look up and wave, "Hey Grey Mars!" they called. Mars took Julian by the shoulder, pulled him close, "She's here. It's gonna happen. Try and relax. God I've never felt better. Hey, how were the caves?"

"Dark, and muddy. Interesting guide. I liked spending time with Soulful. I can see I have nothing to worry about with him. He's so well grounded. But, it's good to be out in the open. I love the smell of the river, that roar of life," Julian said breathing in deeply. Mars clapped him on the shoulder.

"I grabbed us the perfect campsite, too. Right near this crazy little rapid called Troublemaker. Perfectly named. After we grab a drink, we can go watch the carnage. You hungry?"

"I thought no one was drinking," Julian said.

Mars let out the hyena. "The kids can't drink without I.D. The adults have a locked cooler full of beer and wine. We have to set the example. Otherwise this bunch will grow up much too serious."

"Where's Sky?"

"She went with Li-Si to get her ears pierced. And before you say anything, yes I sent someone with them. I know Li-Si has a stalker. We've all had a talk about the press, and all that bullshit. There is press here and they kayak with cameras on their helmets. Some are so good, I keep inviting them along on runs."

Around the campfire, which was just an empty fire pit full of black ash in the early afternoon. Julian was joined by several of his offspring who shook his hand, or hugged him. After that they exchanged polite inquires and then most more or less ignored him to lie back on low cots or to read. Several sat at the picnic table with him, eating grapes from the bowl on the table talking about how difficult it was to whitewater kayak.

Soulful appeared carrying grocery sacks, "Hey Julian! I brought some food. I'll get some firewood, and ice later. If you don't mind, I'm going to try rafting with this group I met up there."

"I hope you like it," Julian laughed, feeling strong and energetic.

Down the shaded path, Julian had the sense that she was strolling toward him. When he looked up, the shadow of the tree that shaded the campsite became Elita. "Julian!" she called, without trying to hide her pleasure at seeing him. Everyone around them took notice, shifting corners of their mouth, eyebrows lifting and setting down. These kids were at that age when they knew love-crush in first blush. They elbowed each other nodded toward them, dipped their heads together to whisper what everyone already knew.

This all felt very normal to Julian, like he was finally a part of life.

"Are you having a good time?" Julian asked them, just to break into their private world.

"This has to be the best experience!" He was told this time and time again which made him feel proud. No one brought up trekking down to the Amazon jungle or the waterfalls of Mexico to retrace the old route.

"Julian, some of us are having trouble flipping in Troublemaker. Can you come and give us a quick critique?"

"I'm coming, too!" Elita called. "Just let me pull a clean dress on."

It took an hour for everyone to get organized. Julian waited on the bank of the river, just above Troublemaker. There were at least a dozen campers there, set up comfortably in lawn chairs, waiting for the carnage. Someone informed him that there was a webcam above them so people at home could watch, too. The river at this section was wide, with a long, well-defined natural dam of strewn rocks and boulders, and of course, some plants which grew from the riverbed between the rocks. This left one line through this part of the river at extreme river left. Across the river were more forest trees. Most of the river was lined with private houses set way back in case of flood. The woods and river still looked natural, for miles in every direction, the grasses grew, the trees filtered the strong sunlight. Besides his one home, Julian couldn't think of another place he would rather live. He wondered if he should take Mars's advice and buy a second home there.

Several rafts went through to the delighted screams of the occupants. On one raft, the tiny, pigtailed guide steering from the back quadrant was bounced off and what looked like a ten-year-old boy grabbed her by the PFD and pulled her back in while the adults threw their paddles in the air. Kayaker after kayaker passed through the exit either right side up or bottom up. This was a delightful kind of carnage, where no one got seriously hurt, except for the frustrated, bruised egos.

Because Elita had strategically taken the higher ground next to him they were standing shoulder to shoulder, encouraging Julian to readjust his stance so he had to lean into her. It wasn't easy to make leaning uphill look natural, but he did it by using his foot to shovel and roll a large stone under his left foot to brace on.

"Why are some flipping over and not others?" Elita asked. By this time she had her arm looped through his, something he quite liked. People studied them, but even Julian knew they made a striking looking couple. He would have stared, too.

"Why do they keep flipping?" Elita asked.

Julian had been studying it long enough to see the problem.

"Watch what they do with the paddle. They lift it up instead of keeping it propelling them through the water. The paddle has to act like an engine in a rapid, especially one like this."

"Where did you learn to kayak?" Elita asked.

Julian, still too shy to look directly at her said, "You see in Norway, we love skiing. Some see all the rivers as just another form of snow, which it is, of course. But I started canoeing when I was maybe only five years old. From a family I got to know at boarding school, I got to try some whitewater when I was ten or so. After that, I came here to America to go to school and part of their program was whitewater kayaking. I learned as part of my physical education, if you can imagine anything so wonderful. This is the river I love best though. It's beautiful, dependable flow, and no damn bugs flying into your face."

"Here comes our first one!" Elita shouted when a blue face appeared at the entrance to the seemingly innocuous rapid. Julian could see the tension in his body posture.

"Relax! Paddle!" he shouted, trying to get his voice over the roar of the river.

Everyone that flipped managed to roll up cleanly once there were flushed out of the rapid, with one exception and the others chased him down and got him, his boat and paddle to the shore. At the post-mortem, Julian offered his rather stern criticism.

"You have to use your lower body to balance. You feel your edge catch, and then you drop your hip, shift, down river enough to get up. And paddle. You all lift your paddle the minute you catch an edge. Brace on the paddle. Slap it on the water and lean on it, just like you are setting up to roll, only push back. Don't let the water move you. You move yourself through the water."

Elita elbowed him so he tacked on, "Good job."

"I hate that rapid! When you flip right there, you get dragged over this rocky lip. Sucks!" One of them cried in frustration, making Julian smile. Sometimes he thought the actual learning of the sport was better than anything that came after.

"Seems like I enter it perfectly each time," another one added.

"It's a bit like a toilet bowl flush, you enter, the river is squeezed, forming that eddie near us here so it is pushing you against those rocks on the opposite side where you get swept around in the downriver current, but you—all of you-- lift the paddle instead of digging in to plow straight through," Julian told them.

"Paddle," Elita said, but more like she was taking the advice for herself.

Julian told them they were going to go through the rapid at least three more times, or until they stopped flipping inside it, reminding them that each time the focus would be level hips so they could swivel with the changing currents, but focus on moving the boat forward with the paddle. Just paddle!

The kayakers flipped their boats onto their shoulders, and trudged off, water-logged, but staying in full gear because it was just so much easier to leave it on than wrestle wet sticky clothes off and on. They were only walking up a few yards to get back in and go through the rapid again.

"You going to go with me next?" Elita asked. "I've been practicing with Grey."

"Let me watch these kids take another pass, and then we'll put in right below this rapid. I think we should put you in a smaller boat, practice rolling it here in the eddie. And just take a leisurely paddle down. Maybe not focus so much on paddling as on enjoying the river."

"I love that idea," Elita said. "Just prepare to help me out. I flip a lot."

"You won't flip with me," Julian promised her.

That day on the river was gently bouncing over the small wave trains, and practicing rolling in the moving water. Julian knew Elita would be a strong kayaker one day, but it didn't matter then.

"Does this bore you?" She asked him.

"I've never felt more at peace," Julian said. That's when they eddied out and began talking nose to nose, kissing a little. Today, he thought, for the first time, he didn't care so much that he was blue.

"How are the little ones?" Elita asked.

"They all report being happy. Rini says they are enjoying the time, but they are missing their father. She always says stuff like that," Julian added. "They cry when I talk to them." Julian sighed.

"You do know they really think of you as their father. Like Sky and Tauro. Maybe many others, too. Kids want a dad. The little ones do miss you Julian. I can imagine how they are listening for the sound of your call or your car even."

After that, they paddled slowly down the river, talking and laughing.

After the second time Elita flipped over, and rolled up, Julian waited until they could paddle into a still eddie.

"The trick is, when you feel that wobble, lean down stream. You won't flip. I know it feels counter-intuitive, but when you lean upstream, the water piles on the boat and helps you over. So next, let's practice bracing downstream. I'll be right there to catch you so lean out as far as you want, press on the paddle and snap your hips up. Soon you won't need that roll so much."

This was all harder than it sounded, mostly because humans tended to want to go upright rather into a steeper tilt when they had the sense of falling. Elita began to get the hang of it though.

"Don't over extend your shoulder if it pops out—"

Elita nodded, tried again with her elbows locked closer to her sides. Julian could see they would have many days of pleasurable paddling together before she was ready for the next step.

The stupid error near-tragedy happened when Elita's back was turned to the island in the river. Julian warned her to spin around and go river right, but it was by some sick coincidence a small tree wavering on the blowing wind toppled over just then, creating the dangerous strainer. Elita dropped her paddle to shield her face and went into it flipping at once. Her boat was trapped.

Julian paddled as close as he could, ripped open the spray skirt, shucked off the PFD so he could get swim under her boat to get her. In the time it took to prepare to dive he saw her helmet pop to the surface. She was laying back across the boat, chin up. He pulled her out and kicked them both to the surface. By the time they hit air, there were other kayakers there pulling her limp body up across a dark boat.

That paddler parted the river to get her to the shore.

Julian swam hard to get to the shore at the same time as the rescue boat.

"I got a de-fib!" A man in a raft called, following.

Elita sat up, wobbling on one bent arm. "I'm breathing. Don't let them do anything to me. Oh Julian, I'm so sorry." She lay back down letting both arms fall straight out, making herself into a cross.

"I'm a nurse. Let me look," someone else said from behind. This woman knelt down and smoothed the hair out of Elita's face as she took up her wrist.

"She's a doctor," Julian said, like that would bring down the healing magic.

"She's breathing. Her pulse is strong. She must be a runner. It's shock. Let's warm her up." A foil blanket was unfolded by someone in Julian's periphery. The nurse rolled her onto her side, and wrapped her up and sat down so their backs touched. "Just give her a few minutes to warm up. The paramedics are coming. You did everything right, Blue Man."

Julian gathered Elita's head into his lap, and silently cried into her wet hair.

Sky somehow materialized as the paramedics took Elita away.

"Dad! Don't worry, she's going to be okay. I should have been here with you."

"No," Julian said. "No, no, no. Don't take any of this on. You were having fun with your sister."

"She's sitting up and talking," the nurse who had been so helpful told him. "Come on, she wants you."

"Sky, I'm going to try to get her to marry me. I don't want you to be a pill about this," Julian told her.

"I'll behave, I promise," Sky wrapped her arms around his waist and leaned so hard into him it was difficult to walk.

"Run back and tell everyone she is sitting up and talking," Julian said. "She might not want everyone down here keeping a vigil."

"Got it!" Sky called, and she let him go, but Julian knew she would stand right where she was until he emerged and joined her again.

"Come along then," he called to her. Sky ran to him, taking his hand.

During the dinner that night, Julian, buoyed by Elita's rapid recovery, stopped feeling self-conscious and guilty, and finally looked up at the other women, the mothers of some of his off spring, the true parents, those who had done the real work. Some also had children that shared their own skin color; some only had the one, blue child. They all seemed to like talking with him. This was very important to Julian. He was careful to never apologize for giving them blue children, because he refused to make it seem like they were less perfect because of it. The imperfect one was Julian. Of course he wished he had known more of them much earlier in their childhood, he regretted that. The mothers agreed they should have tried, too. There was always just so much fear.

Now that he was over coming his reticence, he was beginning to see them as individuals. Debbie, blonde, very funny, she was often accused of having no filter, but that wasn't true, she had the perfect filter of a natural comedian, Julian was certain she made more money in her chosen profession, but he felt the world missed out on what could have been a superb comedic actress. Li-Si's mother was there, Portia, a softer version of her daughter, but just as determined to learn to kayak. Tula-short for the God-awful Petula (her words) was some sort of hydrologist, knew all about the river, and what she affectionately referred to as the riparian environment. And Sandi, Mars's favorite for reasons Julian didn't quite understand. The shy, smart, very practical woman was not his type, at all. Sandi had three cameras, and would only raft. And she regularly beat Mars at cards. There were various other family members that came and went, it was hopeless to think Julian could keep track of all of them, but Sandi promised him a photo album with names, locations and the like, something that would not go online.

Soulful showed up, escorted by Sky and Li-Si and several others, so he knew the story, but he only gave Julian his customary greeting, and another bag of food.

"Fresh fruit and avocados," he told Julian.

"Is this to cover the scent of an In and Out burger?" Julian asked making Soulful laugh. He offered Julian the car keys. "Keep them, you can drive home with Sky. I'll drive with Elita."

Tauro who was as excellent in a kayak as he was in a fistfight, was with a group on a more challenging part of the river. He was in the last group to arrive. While the paramedics were looking her over, Elita made Julian swear he would not to tell Tauro anything until she spoke with him first.

"I'm not giving this up, Julian!" she informed him. "And that boy is not going to guilt me out of trying again. I just learned an important lesson today, that's all that happened. I put you in danger by being too arrogant, and flirting. I love being on the river with you, and I love my little yellow boat." Julian didn't have the heart to tell her the boat was gone, maybe it was wedged somewhere, maybe in the back of someone's truck, maybe taking a ride down the gorge, flushing through those famous rapids.

When Tauro arrived, he was funneled over to her tent where she was reading a magazine, resting with a glass of wine.

"Here's your boy," Julian said as lightly as he could, and then he backed off. An hour later Tauro snuck up behind Julian and grabbed him into the customary hug. "Pa!" Was all he said before setting him down and patting his back. "Did you lose all the gear?" He quietly asked.

"I don't care about that stuff. Plenty more at the store down the road." This is when Tauro openly wept.

"I had a great day," he told Julian. "This is the best possible end. If you're okay, I'm gonna hit the shower."

Julian told him he was better than okay, waited until he was over the horizon, grabbed a bottle of beer and then went to go sit with Elita in her tent, try to find out what she told Tauro about the two of them, if anything.

# Chapter Sixteen

As everyone was cobbling the huge communal dinner together, Grey Mars, hanging onto a tall can of beer like it was keeping him upright, had pulled Julian aside and without preamble said, "Listen never propose to a woman when you're drunk. And don't fucking ever propose to a woman without a ring."

"If no ring than what happens?" Julian asked, humoring Mars.

"Oh, Juli, certain death. Get a ring and keep it in your pocket at all times. You never know when you're going to need it. I got one you can borrow in case you think you might lose your head."

"Thank you, my friend. I don't plan to ruin this by proposing too soon," Julian told him. The hungry hyena shot out of Mars and then he went quiet. Tears gathered in his eyes, he wiped his nose on the tail of his shirt, exposing that scarred belly.

"I so want you happy, Juli," Mars said and then he turned his usual clap on the shoulder into an uncharacteristically huge bear hug. It was then that Julian realized Mars was really drunk, and also how he got himself into so many stupid relationships. Teetering on the edge of drunken-overly-affectionate Mars was where Julian liked to leave him to the women. He slipped out of his hug and went looking for Elita. The brief kiss they had earlier was just not enough.

"Pa!" Tauro cried scooping him into his customary hug in which both feet are lifted off the ground.

"Tauro I want to marry your mother. I'm going to find her now to get started on convincing her," Julian said right into his ear since they were already so close anyway. Tauro dropped him out of the hug at those words, "after you my father!" He shouted before he made a war-whoop.

While Julian was rummaging around in the adults' ice cooler, trying to decide between grabbing two beers or the small bottle of vodka and a bag of the crystal rocks of ice Soulful had thoughtfully brought from the store, Elita wove their fingers in his saying, "Tauro said you were about to go find me."

164

"I was getting us a drink," he smiled at the blackness of Elita's fingers grasping his blue hand.

"I got some agave tequila, the real deal, salt and limes," she whispered. "So come on!"

Julian dropped the beers back in and let her tug him away to a secluded spot at the river edge. She chose the spot and helped him nestle in very close to her. In her lap was a basket that she began pulling the goods out of.

"I forgot to cut the limes," she said, dropping her hands in her lap, like she ruined the best surprise of that basket.

"Hand me one."

When she did he bit it in half. "Here you go," he said.

They had each had a shot from a plastic cup. Julian immediately relaxed and hoped she would offer him another, he felt like losing his head that night. Some evening paddlers went by in a full raft, whooping now that they were out of the quiet zone. Julian told her about his father eating a whole lemon that first night he and Grey Mars met him. The other bits and pieces he stumbled over when he was trying to fill them in, but she leaned into him and whispered, "Grey told me enough about it. You know nothing could get Rini to divulge anything about you except you had a big heart that needed filling. My point is, don't go anywhere in the past if it will spoil this time we're having together right now."

"Good," Julian said, embarrassed. "Good. Good." They sat listening to the river, the people in the campground celebrating the outdoors, many his people. Knowing their voices as well as their faces now made him feel knitted to them in a very spiritual way. The sun set completely leaving them in a haze of that near dark of the summer night. If he had a candle he would light it just to see the details of Elita's beautiful face.

"At night, the river is so noisy isn't it?" She laughed. "I keep waking up at night wondering when someone was going to shut the damn television off. But I never want to leave. I know we have to, but I would like to just stay here forever."

Julian moved in and kissed her. When she kissed back, they leaned into each other. By some signal they broke away reluctantly and drank another shot.

"This feels right to me."

"Yes," Julian said. "Like I've been waiting---"

"Before it goes any farther, I have to be honest with you about some things," Elita said. Julian became very still, but he wanted that bottle and badly for fortification if this was going to be a crushing rejection.

"I can't have more children. Everything went wrong with Tauro, so well, now I'm sterile."

Julian started laughing, before he realized she was serious.

"You're serious! I have sufficient children, Elita. And technically, we do have a son together. A good one, too."

"But you see Julian, I feel cursed. My whole intention, and this is hard for me to say this. I have never told anyone. I am so, so black. I am truly black. Like National Geographic African on the savannah black. And as you know, color matters, maybe even more to people of color. I grew up getting so much grief for this skin. I used to try all sorts of powder to cut it down to a dull brown. You can't believe what a hindrance it has been to be the color of a ironstone pot. Even my own family puts me at the bottom. I'm a doctor and that's not enough. My point is I cursed myself for my vanity. For wanting something by using a short cut. I got into that study because I wanted a white father for my baby. I wanted him to be strong, and healthy true, but really I just wanted to take down this color. They said you were Norwegian, I couldn't imagine anyone whiter. Do you see what I've done?" Elita asked.

"You made Tauro." Julian bit another lime in half, held out his paper cup. "Hit me," he said.

After he drank down the inch she poured him and sucked the lime he said, "I collect black things now. All this color." He held up her hand. "And I think you know my deep affection for Tauro." Saying the word "love" was still nearly impossible for Julian. "So are you really saying that you may want me, as long as we don't have more children together?" Julian asked.

"No!" Elita said. "No, I'm just trying to explain to you about my curse. I'm an educated woman, but this is where my people come from. We are superstitious. It is so ingrained."

"My mother felt she was cursed, too. I think she may have been. My people have their own little demons." Julian took another drink and told her about his vision of her visiting him, and then in the cave that memory or hallucination, and her blue dolls.

"I collect black cloth dolls, the same color as me," Elita said. "I call them my sisters."

"That's what my mother called hers."

"Why is skin color so defining? Was she blue?" Elita asked.

"The last time I saw my father, he told me I turned just like her. I thought he meant the way I was repelled by him, but now I wonder if he was talking color. Could it be possible? I don't remember. It's been too long now."

Elita smiled, "I just want us to be possible."

"Stay," Julian whispered. "I promise I will love you forever."

By the time they stumbled quietly back into Elita's tent, everyone was asleep, but they were too overwhelmed with tequila, and each other to do anything more than collapse on the sleeping bags and pass out in each other's arms.

At breakfast that morning, everyone knew they were as good as engaged, and this being the last night for most everyone, put all the women in high gear. The kayakers were already out getting the shuttles organized so they could wait at the various put ins for the water level to rise high enough to do their last runs. All this was discussed over coffee and cornflakes with peaches, which taking Elita's lead, Julian tried to pretend was more interesting than the contours of her being.

"We are planning a big party tonight," the mom's told Julian. "So you two go spend the day together, and leave it all to us. We will have everything ready!"

Julian and Elita put on the river while most everyone watched, cheering them on. This time she chose a blue boat. For the first mile he stayed so close, before she could slip on an edge, he had his boat bracing hers. They went into eddies, the usual place new kayakers flipped, like one boat he was so close to her.

"Julian! Let me be. I've got to work through this. I want to," she laughed. "You keep saying, just let's relax and have fun, but you look so tense."

"I'm trying to relax," Julian said.

"Okay I'm going to paddle into the current and practice rolling," she said.

"Let me get down below you, in case you need a T-rescue," he said.

"I'm not gonna miss this roll!"

They went on like that, slowly meandering down the river until they got to the take out where the shuttle was waiting.

That night, while Julian showered, the women organized the feast, keeping him out of the main campground until they called him.

When, at last, he arrived, Sky, dressed like a wild woman in some sort of tiki garb, sat him next to Elita in two crazily decorated lawn chairs. Li-Si put a crown of leaves on their head.

That's when the drumming started, and the women emerged painted from head to toe in dark shades of green, blue, purple, pink, their hair in all manner of wildness. Elita started to laugh.

"Julian! A bad little, drunken bird once told us that you often said we fecund bitches should put on the blue skin and get out in the world and see how it felt. We agreed---"

Julian was going to crush Grey Mars the minute he could get his hands on him, but Elita started laughing and laughing. She leaned into him, "they got him really drunk, and got him to open up. Someone promised him some pretty naughty treatment if he would give them a really good line to use."

And then the women opened their circle and there was Grey Mars painted blue, in a grass skirt, and doing some sort of dance that made Julian laugh although he secretly hoped it was made of poison oak.

After that, the kids and painted women declared all of them a new tribe, and then they all went a little wild. People from other camps started to drift over.

"I really want to laugh," Julian said to Elita, looking for guidance.

"I really want to dance with you and them," she told him.

And that's what they did.

**The end.**

Made in the USA
Charleston, SC
12 December 2014